THE CHARLESTON YEARS

The Threat

Nancy Rue

BETHANY HOUSE PUBLISHERS
MINNEAPOLIS

Published by Bethany House Publishers
A Ministry of Bethany Fellowship International
11300 Hampshire Avenue South
Minneapolis, Minnesota 55438

Printed in the United States of America by
Bethany Press International, Minneapolis, Minnesota 55438

Library of Congress Cataloging-in-Publication Data

Rue, Nancy N.
  The threat / Nancy Rue.
      p.   cm. — (The Christian heritage series, the Charleston years ; bk. 3)
    Summary: In 1861, eleven-year-old Austin travels with his family from their
South Carolina plantation to their North Carolina vacation home where he
uncovers a plot against his uncle who opposes secession.
    ISBN 1-56179-566-6
    [1. Family life—Southern States—Fiction. 2. Christian life—Fiction.
3. Southern States—Fiction. 4. Slavery—Fiction.] I. Title. II. Series: Rue,
Nancy N. Christian heritage series, the Charleston Years ; bk. 3.
PZ7.R88515Tl   1998
[Fic]—dc21   97–51659
                                                                          CIP
                                                                           AC

98 99 00 01 02 03 04 / 12 11 10 9 8 7 6 5 4 3 2 1

For Susie Cole,
a treasure I have only just discovered

Canaan Grove Plantation,
Charleston
1860-1861

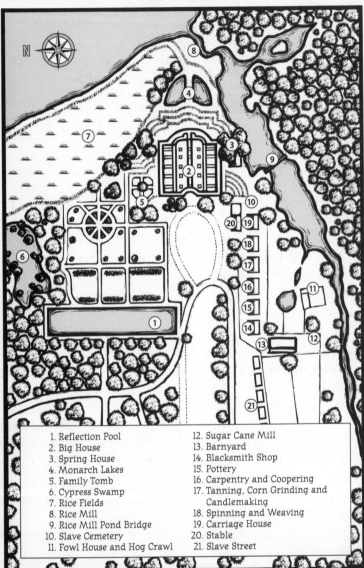

1. Reflection Pool
2. Big House
3. Spring House
4. Monarch Lakes
5. Family Tomb
6. Cypress Swamp
7. Rice Fields
8. Rice Mill
9. Rice Mill Pond Bridge
10. Slave Cemetery
11. Fowl House and Hog Crawl
12. Sugar Cane Mill
13. Barnyard
14. Blacksmith Shop
15. Pottery
16. Carpentry and Coopering
17. Tanning, Corn Grinding and Candlemaking
18. Spinning and Weaving
19. Carriage House
20. Stable
21. Slave Street

"Austin! Come over here and put your head in this clamp! We're all waiting for you!"

Austin Hutchinson pulled his head with its deer-colored hair out of the big box on the back of the wagon and looked over his shoulder. The Ravenals and his mother were all watching him from the front steps of the plantation mansion.

"Come on, young'un!" his Uncle Drayton said again. He nodded his handsome head firmly toward the group that was squinting impatiently into the sun. But he wasn't gritting his teeth yet, so Austin knew he could squeeze out at least another minute.

"I was just checking to see what kind of photography he's doing," Austin called back to his uncle. He craned his neck to see inside the wagon again. "Just as I thought— ambrotype. He has enough collodion in here for a *thousand* photographs! That'll keep the chemicals from sliding off the glass while the plate's being exposed—"

"It's never going to *be* expired if you don't get over here!"

1

That came from 13-year-old Polly, who was sighing and rolling her mud-colored eyes and trying to toss her curls, though as usual they lay like wilted daisy stems at the base of her neck.

"I'm tired of standing here with my head in this *thing!*" she whined on.

"It will steady your pose during the exposure," Austin said as he joined the group. "And it's *exposed*, not *expired*."

"*What* is he talking about?" said Aunt Olivia. With her plump, bejeweled fingers, she dabbed fretfully at the sweat glowing on her nose. "I never understand half of what that boy is saying. Mousie, I need my handkerchief!"

A black woman, who was so small she looked as if she would blow away if a summer breeze kicked up, scurried over and pulled a hanky out of Aunt Olivia's glove and began to mop her brow with it. Beside Austin, there was a groan from Kady, who had just turned 17.

"As if Mama couldn't have done that herself," she muttered.

A shriveled, completely bald man pulled his head out from under the black cloth that covered the camera. "All right, is everyone ready?" he asked.

"I hope *he* is," whispered a voice behind Austin.

He grinned back at his cousin Charlotte—11 years old like him and practically his twin, except that her fawn-colored hair cascaded down her back, while his was cropped close around his ears and hung in a wispy fringe across his forehead. They both had golden-brown eyes, like Austin's mother and Charlotte's father, and the Ravenal turned-up nose, which now in early summer was covered in twice as many freckles as usual.

"Last spring when he tried to take our photograph,"

Charlotte whispered, "he nearly set himself on fire."

"Which is why we have to do it again now," Kady hissed. "And I wish he would get on with it." She glared down at the miles of lace that surrounded her pale pink gown. "I'm barbecuing in this thing."

"I think we're all here now," Uncle Drayton trumpeted out in his silvery voice.

"Oh, no," someone else said.

They all pulled their heads out of their clamps to look up at Austin's mother, Sally Hutchinson, who was on the top row next to her brother Drayton.

"What's wrong, sweet potato pie?" Uncle Drayton said to her.

"Jefferson isn't here," she said.

There was a chorus of moans.

"Of *course* he isn't!" Aunt Olivia said shrilly. "That child is *never* where he's supposed to be. Drayton, we have packing to do!"

And we have playing to do, Austin thought. Henry-James had the afternoon off, and he and Charlotte and Austin had plans for their last day together before they left Henry-James for Flat Rock.

Austin looked around for his slave friend. He knew he was somewhere around because he could hear Bogie, his bloodhound-mutt, baying happily.

"Well, where *is* the little man?" Uncle Drayton was saying. He continued to smile his charming, unruffled grin, but Austin could hear in his voice that he was quickly growing weary of this whole thing.

"I don't know," Mother said. "He was here just a moment ago."

"He's probably under one of our skirts," Polly said. She

squealed and swished her six feet of crinoline. "What was that? Tot, check under my petticoats—that's where he likes to hide!"

Polly's stump-shaped slave girl lumbered toward them, but she tripped—over nothing, as far as Austin could see— and Sally Hutchinson said, "Austin, would you please go look for your brother?"

"Why don't we just go on without him?" Aunt Olivia said.

"Because this is a *family* portrait," Uncle Drayton said through his teeth. "I want the *whole* family here."

"Me, too!" chirped a little voice at the front door of the Big House. "That's why I went up after this!"

Once again, all heads turned—while the bald photographer sighed dramatically and threw up his hands. Six-year-old Jefferson Hutchinson was emerging from the house, dressed in his pale blue velvet suit with a huge bow at his throat and clutching a flat, square object against his chest ruffles.

"What do you have there, my love?" Mother said.

Jefferson flipped open what he was carrying and displayed both it and his deep dimples. "Father's picture," he said. "He should be in the photograph, too."

"Bless his heart," Kady murmured.

"Oh, for heaven's sake," Aunt Olivia said, flapping her lace fan testily in her face. "You'll never be able to see it—"

"Wonderful, little man!" Uncle Drayton said gaily. "I would be honored to have Wesley Hutchinson in our family photo."

Austin could see Aunt Olivia's double chins stiffening like beaten egg whites.

She sure wouldn't, Austin thought. *She hates Father.*

Jefferson wriggled into place beside him, and the dark-haired, blue-eyed, chunky child dimpled up at Austin and proudly unfolded the brass miniature case against his ruffles. Austin looked down at it, and to his own surprise, his chest pinched.

He hadn't seen his father's serious face for six months. And except for a few times, he hadn't really missed him much. There was so much to do here at Canaan Grove, and he'd had so many adventures since he'd been here. But now, looking at the solemn eyes and remembering that they were blue just like Jefferson's . . . seeing the dark hair, combed but still looking tousled, the way Jefferson's always did . . . and watching the lips, expecting them to launch into a lecture about the evils of slavery—

Now, suddenly, Austin missed him.

"If we are all in *place*," the photographer said, nervously twiddling his thumbs.

Uncle Drayton nodded, and everyone put their heads back into their clamps. Jefferson started to whine, but Austin poked his shoulder and he hushed up. The photographer lunged under the black cloth again and peered at them from the back of his camera.

Austin knew he was adjusting his lens to focus their image reflected on a special glass before his eyes. He'd read all about photography while traveling with his abolitionist parents. Since he'd spent most of his life—until January, when he came Canaan Grove—on trains and steamers and in hotels and lecture halls, he'd read all about almost everything.

The bald man pulled his head out from under the cloth and squinted anxiously at the group. "Could the young missy with the wide skirt—could she flatten that down just a bit? It's hiding most of the lady behind her."

Polly sniffed haughtily and started to squash down her crinolines, but Aunt Olivia said, "Who is behind her?"

"Sally," Uncle Drayton said.

"She can't be covering her that much." Aunt Olivia tossed the silk net that held her dark hair in a bunch at the nape of her neck. "Please, let us get on with the photo."

"But we want a picture-perfect moment, ma'am," the photographer said. His thumbs were twiddling madly.

"It's really all right," Sally Hutchinson said. Austin could hear the laughter nudging at her voice.

The photographer nodded reluctantly and snapped his fingers. From the back of the wagon, a skinny boy appeared, carrying something in a wooden carrier.

"The sensitized glass negative," Austin whispered. "That's a lightproof carrier it's in."

"Hush up, Boston Austin," Polly hissed back. She was using the nickname she'd given him. She always called him that when she thought he was acting like a know-it-all northern professor-type. "None of us cares. We want to get on with the packing!"

"So she can get to Flat Rock and start flirting with the boys," Kady muttered under her breath.

There was much pulling away of carriers and slides, and then the photographer called out, "Hold the pose!"

Austin suddenly had the urge to look like Father in the picture. He made his face serious and his eyes big, and he stared solemnly into the camera. For the first time since Father had left that January morning—so that Austin's sickly mother Sally Hutchinson could rest while he went on with his anti-slavery lectures and writings—Austin thought, *I want him to be proud of me.*

"One thousand nine," the photographer called out

excitedly. "One thousand *ten!* Release the pose!"

There was a collective sigh of relief as the photographer popped the cap over the lens and the plate was slid back into its carrier and swept off to the wagon.

"Come on, Austin," Charlotte said from behind him. "Let's change our clothes and go meet Henry-James."

As they climbed the stairs to his room on the second floor, Austin said, "You're sure Henry-James doesn't have to work this afternoon?"

It was his mother who answered from behind. She was headed for her bedroom across from his, her face white from a whole morning of being up and about.

"That's right," she said. "Lay-by time, when the rice has all been hoed and the final flood has been let into the fields. There isn't as much for the slaves to do until harvest— otherwise they would be out there in this heat and humidity, just like they are every other day."

She's feeling better, Austin thought.

Mother didn't usually say much here about the slavery she had hated since she was a little girl growing up at Canaan Grove. But lately, with Henry-James's mother, Ria, taking care of her and the rest giving her strength and energy, she was speaking up more. It didn't make Aunt Olivia very happy.

But then, nothing besides new furniture and new dresses makes Aunt Olivia happy, Austin thought.

"Hurry up and change your clothes," Charlotte said, tugging at his blue velvet sleeve. "This will be our last day to play before we leave for Flat Rock."

She skipped off down the hall. Austin frowned at his mother.

"I don't see why we have to leave Canaan Grove for the

rest of the summer," he said. "I like it here."

"Trust me, you don't want to be here during the rice-growing," Mother said. "Haven't you smelled the standing water already? It's a wretched stench. Not to mention the swarms of mosquitoes. There's no worse time for malaria."

"But the slaves have to stay here," Austin said.

"Right—to simmer in their misery. And a lot of them get very sick from this disease-ridden heat. It's brutal."

It was her turn to frown. She slipped into her room and shut the door.

Austin sagged as he went into his own room. He pulled on light pantaloons and a loose shirt and was picking up Jefferson's velvet suit off the floor when he heard a voice outside the window.

"Massa Austin!" someone was calling.

Austin flung himself to the window and hung halfway out. A black face with round black eyes and a wonderful space between two front teeth looked up at him. Sweat glistened on the 13-year-old's close-cropped black hair.

"Henry-James!" Austin said.

"You gon' stay up there all day changin' your clothes?" Henry-James said.

"I'll be right down!" Austin called to him. "Meet me at the back door!"

He took the back stairs two at a time and was sliding across the wide, elegant hall to the door when he heard Uncle Drayton's library door open and breathed in his uncle's leather-and-lavender smell.

"Austin," he said, "would you step in here for a moment, please? I have something for you."

Austin looked anxiously at the door. "Can you wait just a minute while I tell Henry-James where I am?"

Uncle Drayton's eyebrows pointed up like arrowheads. "He is a *slave*, Austin. *He* will wait."

Austin looked out the window by the door. He could see Henry-James standing in the shade of a poplar. Sighing, Austin followed his uncle into the library, but he felt annoyed as he went, as if something were poking him.

"The stagecoach brought mail this morning," Uncle Drayton said when Austin had slipped into the book-lined mahogany room. "There's something here for your mother—and something for you."

"Me?" Austin said. He eyed the lumpy envelope curiously.

"It came from Rochester, New York," Uncle Drayton said. "We can only suppose it's from your father."

ustin felt his eyes spring open wide. "Father sent a letter just to *me?*"

"I don't know any other 'Master Austin Hutchinson'," Uncle Drayton said. He smiled his charming smile as he handed the packet to Austin. "You may open it here if you like, while I open my mail." His eyes sparkled. "And then we had better get packing or Aunt Olivia will have *us* thrown into a trunk."

Austin's fingers shook as he ripped open the envelope flap. There was a folded piece of paper inside—and something gold. Austin pulled it out and cradled it in his palm.

It was an American flag, only about an inch long but perfectly detailed with stars and stripes painted on. On the back was a pin.

Austin unfolded the letter. Knowing Father, there would be an explanation—a long one—inside. The letter said:

Dear Son,
It is my hope that you will receive this before you leave

for your summer in the mountains. I know you will be surrounded there by people who believe that this nation must be split in half so that slavery may be continued. I want you to wear this—proudly—as a reminder of how wrong that is. Please remember what is important, what I must be away from you to fight for. And pray that very soon it will all be resolved and we may be a family again. Be safe. Godspeed.

Father

Austin read the letter three times before he folded it and returned it to its envelope. Then he stared down at the shiny pin in the palm of his hand—and deep in his chest, he ached to be with his father.

He doesn't know how tall I've gotten. He doesn't know I actually have friends now. Austin felt his throat get tight. *I wish Father were here right now. Uncle Drayton is nice to me, but it isn't the same. I can't even show him this pin—because he doesn't* believe *in what it stands for.*

He closed his fingers over the pin and looked anxiously across the mahogany desk at his uncle. Drayton Ravenal was poring over his mail, and his tanned face was pale and drawn. His eyes glared at the paper.

"Who is your letter from?" Austin said.

Uncle Drayton's head came up, and for a moment he looked as if he had forgotten Austin was there.

"It's just business," he said briskly. He folded the letter and stuffed it back into the envelope. He formed a smile with his mouth, but it didn't reach his eyes. "Shall we get to work?"

The only thing I want to do is show this to Charlotte and Henry-James! Austin thought. As soon as Uncle

Drayton gave him the nod, he shot from the room, nearly bowling over Aunt Olivia, who was on her way in. Her chins quivered as she shook her head at him, and she shut the library door behind her.

Charlotte was waiting impatiently for Austin in the hall.

"What took you so long?" she said, pushing him toward the back door.

Austin felt the pin still in his hand. "Something I have to show you and Henry-James. Let's go someplace where nobody can hear us."

"But don't forget," she said. "We can't go off the plantation with Henry-James. You know how bad the Patty Rollers want to get him."

Austin shuddered as he remembered thin-bearded Barnabas Brown with his nasty tobacco breath and balding Irvin Ullmann, whose voice sounded like a heel grinding in gravel. They patrolled St. Paul's Parish constantly, looking for slaves who were off their plantations without a written pass from their masters. If they found one—especially Henry-James—they would do terrible things to him first and then return him to his master for a reward.

The only things worse than the Patty Rollers, Austin thought as he pinned the flag inside the waistband of his pantaloons, *are those two men from Charleston who—*

But Charlotte suddenly grabbed Austin's wrist. Her brown eyes grew wide as dinner plates. "Listen!" she said.

Austin cocked his head. Sure enough, angry voices were spilling out from the cracks around the library door. Austin nodded to Charlotte, and they both skittered under one of the two sets of stairs in the back hall and listened—just as they had done so many times before.

"It wasn't bad enough that you received mail for Sally

from New York," Aunt Olivia was saying, her voice stretched like a piece of piano wire. "The stagecoach driver will have that all over Charleston by tomorrow."

"Everyone in Charleston knows about Wesley—"

"But now you're getting threatening letters!"

"One!"

"That is one too many!" Aunt Olivia cried. "I have told you until I am blue in the face, it is dangerous for us to have that abolitionist woman and her children living under the same roof with us."

"That 'abolitionist woman' is my sister," Uncle Drayton said, his voice pulling tight, too. "And this has nothing to do with her. This is about my refusal to go along with those Fire Eater secessionists." Austin knew exactly who Uncle Drayton was talking about. The Fire Eaters were men who believed so strongly that the South should separate from the North that people said they breathed fire when they talked about it. Austin had practically seen them do it. "They would have South Carolina secede from the Union the minute Abraham Lincoln is elected," his uncle was saying.

"*If* he is!"

"Don't be silly, Olivia. With the mess the South has made of the Democratic Party—splitting it all asunder the way they did last spring—anyone who runs for the Republicans would win. Jefferson Hutchinson could become President!"

Charlotte poked Austin and grinned.

"Rhett and Chesnut and Pryor—they have threatened to make my life miserable if I do not go along with their plan," Uncle Drayton went on. "Anyone who does not conform these days in the South is very unpopular."

Austin almost called out, "That's right!"

He and Charlotte and Henry-James had met up with two

of the secessionists last spring—tall Mr. Rhett with his one big eyebrow and squatty Mr. Chesnut, who flared his nostrils and wheezed through his yellow teeth. Meeting up with them had given Austin his biggest scare ever.

"Then I see nothing for you to do but go along with them, Drayton," Aunt Olivia said flatly.

"I will do nothing of the kind!"

"You always have before!"

"Before, I was a different man than I am now. I have learned a great deal these last months."

"Since your sister came here and began to infect this house with her ideas."

"Enough! I have a mind of my own, and I will thank you to remember that! I believe we can settle our differences with the North without seceding. You know what that would do—we would be at war within the day!"

"Say what you want, Drayton," said Aunt Olivia. Austin could imagine her double chins trembling angrily. "But having the Hutchinsons here is not helping. That Austin alone has drawn more attention to us than—"

"All right, since you can think of nothing else," Uncle Drayton said, just as angrily, "I can assure you that after a summer of our being away, everyone in Charleston will have forgotten that my sister and her boys even exist. By the time we return, it will have blown over, and hopefully these southern Fire Eaters will have come to their senses about secession as well. In the meantime, it will be a summer without troubles."

"I hope you're right," Aunt Olivia said.

Austin and Charlotte could hear her skirts swishing, and they knew she was standing up to go. Austin pushed Charlotte toward the back door, but they weren't fast enough. Aunt Olivia appeared, red-faced and aquiver.

"Where do you two think you're going?" she said in her shrill, I-mean-business voice.

Charlotte, as usual when it came to her mother, didn't say anything.

Austin cleared his throat. "We have some plans, but I won't bother going into all that," he said, "what with your being so busy and all."

"That is exactly right," Aunt Olivia said. "Now get yourselves upstairs, both of you. Charlotte, pack your clothes. Austin, put all of your little brother's toys that he is taking into the trunk in the nursery. And leave room for Charlotte's dolls and little furniture and tea things."

"Charlotte plays with dolls?" Austin said.

"Not nearly so much as she should."

"Why *should* she?" Austin said.

Aunt Olivia's chins seemed to triple. "We had them imported from England so she can practice being a good mother. By the time Kady and Polly were Charlotte's age, they had both sewn complete wardrobes for their dolls." She tossed her plump hands toward the ceiling, and before Austin could say anything, she had swept away, calling out, "Mousie! Where are you, girl? I don't have time to spend my morning searching all over creation for *you*!"

"Don't pack any of those silly doll things, Austin," Charlotte said fiercely when she was gone. "I'm only taking my stuffed rabbit—the one I sleep with."

"You sleep with a stuffed rabbit?" Austin said. "I never knew that."

"I've had it since I was a baby. It's the only toy I still care about." She shrugged that off. "Now come on—hurry! If we pack soon enough, there might still be time to play."

"There *has* to be," Austin said. "We're not going to see Henry-James for a long time after today!"

Up in the nursery, with Jefferson standing over him, Austin flung toys into the trunk as fast as he could. He was still thinking about Aunt Olivia, and he felt like someone was poking him again, right between the shoulder blades.

My parents never run around screaming at everyone like that, he thought.

"Take the checkers," Jefferson said. "You can teach me to play. Dominoes, too. What about a jigsaw puzzle?"

"What about a punch in the nose?" Austin muttered.

Jefferson stuck his tongue out and went over to the corner. The only toy left out was a rag doll, which he picked up and made a face at.

By the time Austin was finished, the trunk was crammed with wind-up trains, building blocks, whirligigs, tops, pull animals, a miniature fire brigade, and a complete Noah's ark set.

"He never had this many toys before," Austin grumbled. "Where did he get all this stuff?"

"That child has wanted for nothing since Daddy took a fancy to him," Polly said as she sailed past the room. She stopped and looked in suspiciously. "You're not finished with all your jobs, are you?"

Austin slammed the trunk shut. Suddenly, with everyone shoving work at him, he missed his father again. He fingered the pin on his waistband.

"Well," Polly said, "have you got all your things together?"

"The important ones," Austin said. And he felt the pin again. "You're Jefferson's nursemaid. Why didn't *you* have to pack his things?"

Polly's eyes seemed to move closer together. "I will have you know that I am not *anyone's* nursemaid. I am a Ravenal, and therefore I am—"

"A simpleton!" Jefferson said from the corner.

"How incredibly rude!" Polly cried. She turned on Austin as if he himself had said it. "Do you see what I have to put up with, taking care of this little brat every day? I don't know how I'll abide it all summer in the mountains."

"I don't want you taking care of me anyway!" Jefferson said, waving the rag doll. "If you come near me, I'll smash all your curls down with this!"

I don't think her curls need any help being smashed down, Austin wanted to say. He thought better of it, however, as Polly's face turned watermelon red and she flounced toward the door.

Jefferson let fly with the doll and hit her on the back of the head.

When she was gone, with Jefferson running and squealing after her, Austin took the pin off his waistband and attached it to his collar. He was still feeling poked and stubborn—but it wasn't quite so bad now.

The house was alive the rest of the morning with shouts from room to room.

"This trunk is ready!"

"Bring me another bag. I've run out of room!"

"Who took my crinoline? I used to have six. Now I have only five!"

At noon, Isaac, the strongest slave at Canaan Grove, was called in from the stables to carry trunks downstairs where the next day they would be loaded into the wagon for the drive to the train station. He was worked up into a lather of sweat before he got Polly's second trunk down to the back hall. Charlotte and Austin were trying to get out to find Henry-James when Uncle Drayton emerged from his library.

"These are all the ladies' trunks, is that correct?" he said.

"No, sir," Isaac said. "This here just Miz Polly's. Plus she got one to go upstairs."

"What in heaven's name?" Uncle Drayton said. His voice trumpeted up the stairs. "Miss Pumpkin Polly to the back hall, please!"

Polly stomped out of her room. "What *is* it, Daddy? I have packing to do!"

"Merciful heavens, girl. Why do you need three trunks? What is *in* these things?"

"Those are my dresses," she said, pointing to one. "Walking dresses, traveling dresses, some for breakfast, others for dinner and receptions and parties." She stuck her finger out at the other trunk. "And there are shoes in that one."

"Shoes? How many pairs do you need?"

"Mama just had five pairs of balmorals sent in for me from Scotland, and—"

"What's a balmoral?" Austin said.

"Not that it's any of *your* business," Polly said, "but they're all the thing right now. Queen Victoria introduced them in Balmoral, Scotland."

"And you had to have five pairs," Uncle Drayton said.

"Dad-dy! You don't want me to look like a poor white come to Flat Rock, do you? Don't you realize it's the 'Little Charleston of the Mountains'?" She tossed her head as if that didn't even require an answer. "My last trunk will be ready as soon as the darkies have finished ironing my other six gowns. Tot is almost finished packing my hatboxes."

"Hatboxes, too?" Uncle Drayton said. He looked completely baffled. "How many of those?"

"What difference does it make?" Aunt Olivia said, bustling up behind him. "You know she's a young lady now, and young ladies require a great deal of equipment."

"Only when they make a career out of wearing the latest fashions!" Uncle Drayton said. His golden-brown eyes were shining, and Austin thought he actually looked proud.

"Don't distract her," Aunt Olivia said. "She has things to do!"

"Is she going to pack my trunk next?" Uncle Drayton said.

Aunt Olivia looked at him, horrified. "Your trunk?"

"I haven't gotten 'round to finding a new body slave. I've no one to take care of my personal affairs."

"Then you'll have to pack your own trunk," Aunt Olivia said as she hurried toward the door with Mousie scurrying timidly after her.

"Where are *you* off to?" Uncle Drayton said.

"I must oversee the darkies who are finishing up my sewing," she said over her shoulder. "This morning I caught Henrietta dozing when she was supposed to be stitching lace onto one of my day dresses. I made her stand up and sew."

"Of course she was falling asleep," Charlotte whispered to Austin. "They've been sewing day and night for weeks!"

"Does Kadydid have this many trunks?" Uncle Drayton said. "I'm afraid the train won't be able to leave the station!"

Aunt Olivia glared at him and called out, "Kady!"

Kady appeared on the stairs, notebook and pencil in hand.

"What is that for?" Aunt Olivia said.

"I'm working on a poem," Kady said. "But don't worry, Mama, my trunk is all packed."

"Trunk? Just one?"

"Yes," Kady answered. "What's wrong with that?"

"Kady Sarah!" Aunt Olivia cried. She darted up the steps like a startled chicken. "You couldn't possibly have packed everything you're going to need in one trunk!"

"I've brought a few dresses," Kady said, "and some shoes, underwear—"

"Kady Sarah Ravenal!" Aunt Olivia cried, chins trembling in shock. "Genteel people do not speak such a word aloud!"

"What word?" Austin said.

Aunt Olivia glared and turned away.

"Underwear," Charlotte whispered in his ear.

"What are you supposed to call your drawers, then?" Austin whispered back.

"Linens. Unmentionables."

Aunt Olivia marched herself to the back door and flung it open. She was met nose to nose by a man with a wiry beard.

"Excuse me, Miz Ravenal," said Barnabas Brown, the Patty Roller. "Irvin Ullmann and myself, we have something to take up with your husband."

Chapter Three

"**W**hat is it?" Aunt Olivia asked. "Can't you see we're busy here?"

"Yes'm," Barnabas said.

"And I'll thank you to remove your hat in the presence of ladies!"

They both whipped off their floppy felt hats, and Barnabas rolled his up in his hands as he spoke.

"We would really like to speak with *Mr.* Ravenal, ma'am. Seein's how you all are 'bout to leave the plantation and all—"

"Then speak," said Uncle Drayton as he crossed the hall. "And make it brief. I am a busy man."

"We just wanted to reassure you, sir," Barnabas whined, "that while you and your family are gone, we'll keep a real good watch on the place. You won't lose a single darky."

"Fine," Uncle Drayton said. "Will that be all?"

Barnabas looked nervously at Irvin, who growled under his breath.

"Not *all*," Irvin said. "There's one slave in particular we want to warn you about, Mr. Ravenal, and we'll be keeping a specially close eye on him."

Uncle Drayton sighed wearily. "Which one?"

"That young'un right there can tell you," Irvin growled.

All eyes followed his grimy finger to Austin.

"Every time we catch your little darky where he shouldn't oughta be—"

"Or lookin' like he's headin' in that direction," Barnabas put in.

"—that there nephew of yours is with him."

"What is your *point?*" Uncle Drayton said impatiently.

Irvin just growled and poked Barnabas with his elbow.

"Beggin' your pardon, Mr. Ravenal, sir," Barnabas said, "but that there nephew boy is a danger to you and yours—"

"Jus' look at him!" Irvin spewed out. "He struts around here wearin' a Union flag on his collar. He ought to be locked up hisself—locked up with them runaway slaves!"

Austin put a finger up to touch his pin. With so many eyes piercing it, he was sure a hole had been drilled clean through it.

"Where on earth did you get *that?*" Aunt Olivia shrieked.

"Oh, for mercy's sake, Mama," Kady said. "It's the American flag, not the devil's pitchfork!"

"But you know what that means around here!" Olivia said, her voice winding up higher with every word.

"That we're all Americans?" Austin said.

"You hush up!" Aunt Olivia turned on Uncle Drayton like an angry goose. "Do you *see?* His very presence here is an invitation to accuse us of not going along with the rest of the South—"

"Olivia, let me handle this," Uncle Drayton cut her off sharply. He turned to the Patty Rollers, who looked dingy and out of place amid the women's gowns and even Mousie's and Tot's starched white aprons. "I must see to the affairs of my plantation, as I am perfectly capable of doing. Now if you'll excuse me—"

"What about that slave boy?" Irvin growled.

"I will handle it."

Uncle Drayton's glaring eyes drove them away from the back door and down the steps. Then Drayton marched through everyone else, parting the slaves like a comb through hair.

"Where are you going, Drayton?" Aunt Olivia said. Her eyes were almost wild. "What are you going to do about *this* boy?" She flung her ringed hand in Austin's direction.

"What would you *have* me do?" Uncle Drayton said. He stopped at the door and glowered at her. "What must I do before I am allowed to be on about my business?"

"You can begin by telling him to take off that wretched pin."

"Very well!" Uncle Drayton said. He snapped his fingers abruptly. "Austin, please do not wear that pin in public. It upsets your aunt."

"But this is from my father!" Austin said.

"All the more reason, then!" Aunt Olivia cried.

"That isn't fair!"

"Few things are, young Hutchinson," Uncle Drayton said. "Now if there is nothing else, I am going to find Elias and give him his instructions for my absence." He looked at his wife. "I trust you understand that is as important as my nephew's jewelry?"

She sniffed. Uncle Drayton stormed out, and Austin was sure someone was poking him right in the back.

"Well, do it, Austin," Aunt Olivia said. "Take that pin off at once!"

No, I won't! Austin wanted to scream at her. But with shaking fingers, he fumbled at the clasp.

"Oh, Lordy!" a voice suddenly cried from outside. "Miz Polly, help!"

They all rushed out to see stumpy Tot standing stock-still in the middle of the yard with a bucket of water balanced on her head. Her eyes bulged like a frog's as she stared ahead of her and screamed.

"Miz Polly, help! That dog gon' get me!"

The dog in question was Bogie, who bounded toward her, shaking his big head until his ears flopped. And behind him, squealing like a piglet, ran Jefferson—straight at Tot.

Austin bolted for the porch railing. "Jefferson, look out!" he yelled.

But whatever he and Bogie were running from was more powerful than his warning, because they both kept on like two bullets with only one place to go—right into Tot.

As everyone on the porch cried out in unison, Bogie plowed into her first, jerking her legs out from under her. The bucket took flight off her head and dumped on Jefferson as he ran over her like she was one of Aunt Olivia's oriental rugs. The two of them tangled into a squealing knot, and Bogie came back, whining pitifully.

Austin, Kady, and Charlotte dashed toward them, and Uncle Drayton, too, ran their way. But all of them stopped several feet short of the tangled pile of dog and people.

"What is that *smell?*" Austin said, pinching his nostrils shut.

"There's no mistaking *that,*" Uncle Drayton said, backing up. "That's skunk."

Jefferson poked his head out from under the armpit of Tot, who was still wailing as if she were being murdered.

"Me and Bogie cornered him in the woods!" he said. "We woulda caught him, too, if he hadn't stunk everything up!"

Kady picked him up, dripping clothes and all, and then gagged. "You are *rank*, child!" she said. "You're going to need a mud and vinegar bath directly—you *and* the dog!"

"I get to play in mud?" Jefferson said, blue eyes lighting up like two little gas lamps.

"For several hours," Kady said. She scrunched up her nose.

Tot was still moaning, and Uncle Drayton snapped at her to hush up. She did, but she kept clutching her ankle and rocking back and forth.

"Miz Polly," she whimpered.

"Go get Ria, Lottie," Kady said. "I think Tot's sprained her ankle."

"Somebody grab that animal before he contaminates my hounds with that stench," Uncle Drayton said.

Kady glared at him. "Daddy, sometimes you show more concern for those prize hounds than you do for your slaves. This girl is hurt."

"Tot! My Tot!" Polly screeched as she tore toward them from the porch. She smacked Austin out of the way and threw herself on the whimpering slave girl.

If she wasn't hurt before, she is now, Austin thought.

"What happened?" Polly cried. She gave Tot a rough shake. "Tell me what happened!"

"They done run me over!" Tot said in her fingernail-scraping voice. "That dog—and Massa Jefferson."

Polly arched her neck at Jefferson like a queen about to order a beheading.

"You!" she said. "You are nothing but trouble! Daddy, do you see what I'm going to have to put up with all summer?"

"No!" Jefferson screamed back at her. He lurched out of Kady's arms and scrambled to the ground. "I don't want you putting up with me!"

Before anyone could grab him, he charged forward and kicked Polly squarely in the behind. His foot bounced off her thick padding of crinolines, but Polly sent up a squall as if she'd been stabbed. Austin snatched Jefferson up and held him, kicking and shrieking, in his arms. Tot bawled like a lost calf, and even Bogie threw his head back and howled.

"Enough!" Uncle Drayton cried.

There was silence. Austin buried his mouth in Jefferson's hair to keep from laughing, then gagged at the smell and set him down.

"Good heavenly days!" Uncle Drayton said. "I feel as if I'm being pulled at like a cotton boll! I've got the Patty Rollers telling me what to do with Henry-James. I've got my wife telling me to pack my own trunk. I've got my six-year-old nephew and my 13-year-old daughter telling me what the child care arrangements are going to be. I think I'll go mad if I receive one more order!"

"Now you know how the slaves feel," Austin muttered under his breath.

There was a real poke in his back this time—from Charlotte.

"I see only one solution to this," Uncle Drayton said.

Austin stiffened. Uncle Drayton's "solutions" weren't always his favorite thing.

"Henry-James will go with us to the mountains," he said. "Then I can keep an eye on him personally without Brown and Ullmann tearing up Canaan Grove incessantly hunting him. He can look after Jefferson and act as my valet."

"Your valet!" Aunt Olivia called from the porch. Her voice was muffled by the lace handkerchief she held over her nose and mouth. "He's never been a house servant—he's a field hand!"

"I'm sure he can be trained to shine my boots and saddle my horse and bring me my coffee in bed," Uncle Drayton said. "And it's only for the summer."

"I do not approve of this!"

"And I do not care," Uncle Drayton said. "Austin, Charlotte, go find the boy and bring him to me. And Daddy Elias, too."

"Yes, sir!" Austin said. He took off with Charlotte on his heels.

Henry-James hurried off to see Uncle Drayton as soon as Austin and Charlotte delivered the news to him. Austin would have run with him, but he had to go slow with Daddy Elias hobbling beside him.

"The slaves will stay here to simmer in their misery," his mother had said.

The words struck at Austin as they followed Henry-James and he watched Daddy Elias shake the sweat out of the straw hat Ria had made for him.

He has to stay here and suffer while the rest of us go someplace cool, he thought sadly. *And what am I going to do without him all summer?*

He fingered the pin that was still on his collar. No matter how happy most things were, there was always something that wasn't. Daddy Elias was as much a friend to him as Charlotte and Henry-James. Without him, he wouldn't know a thing about Jesus, and without his stories and wise advice, he wasn't sure he could use what he did know.

But when they reached the house, it sounded like there were children who had no troubles at all. Every slave child at Canaan Grove seemed to be gathered in a squealing bunch around a two-horse buggy that was drawn up in the circular front drive with a drummer—a traveling sales-man—leaning against it.

Towering over all of them, Uncle Drayton stood in the middle of the sea of shiny black faces and reaching arms. The buggy behind him had two trunks that were overflow-ing with trinkets—tops and jacks, tiny circus animals on wheels and painted wooden dolls small enough to fit into your hand. Little boats and train cars and bags of marbles spilled out, teasing the delighted children below.

Shadows fell across Austin's mind as he watched. *That's kind of mean*, he thought. *Uncle Drayton is going to buy trinkets for Charlotte and me and Jefferson from that drummer—and all the slave children are going to watch.*

At once, Austin got the poking feeling again. Uncle Dray-ton might have changed—like he had told Aunt Olivia today in the library—but he still did some things Austin didn't understand.

Well, Austin told himself, *if he buys anything for me, I'm going to say no thank you.*

"All right now," Uncle Drayton trumpeted out just then. "Each of you may pick what you like, but no pushing and grabbing. You all know your manners."

"Yes, marse!" they cried in unison.

And then every pair of arms went down to the sides of each knee-length shirt and stayed there, straight and trem-bling, while Uncle Drayton picked up a small girl with braids all over her head and lifted her up to the buggy.

"Choose a toy," he said.

The little crowd waited breathlessly as she pointed to a wooden doll and the drummer handed it to her. She gazed at it as if it were a gold piece as Uncle Drayton set her down and picked up the next wide-eyed slave child.

Austin watched with his mouth gaping open as each of the 40 children was presented with a trinket and stared at it, starry-eyed.

"Is that everyone?" Uncle Drayton said as he put the last child on the ground.

"What 'bout Henry-James?" one of the children lisped.

Henry-James was lurking at the edge of the crowd. He ducked his head and waved them off with his hand.

"Why doesn't he get something?" Austin whispered to Charlotte.

"Because he isn't a child anymore, since he turned 13 this year. He works in the fields now." Charlotte's brown eyes looked sad. "It must be hard your first year not getting a present."

Henry-James was obviously trying to make it *look* as if it were not hard. He kept waving the children off as they jumped up and down around him and shouted, "Henry-James! Henry-James!"

"Well, now, Henry-James," Uncle Drayton said—a little stiffly, Austin thought. "It seems these children will never be satisfied unless I break my rule and buy you a trinket, too."

"You don' need to be doin' that, Marse Drayton," Henry-James said.

"If you are going to be my body slave for the summer, you will learn not to tell me what I need to be doing." Uncle Drayton's voice was wooden.

Austin felt Charlotte grow rigid beside him, and he caught his breath.

"Here," Uncle Drayton said. He picked up a tiny figure of a brown dog and handed it to Henry-James. "This looks like that smelly mutt of yours. Perhaps you'll like this."

There was to be no "perhaps" about it. Henry-James took the dog, said a clear, "Thank you, Marse Drayton," and then waited until Uncle Drayton turned away before he moved.

Just like a good slave boy, Austin thought bitterly. But his thoughts chased off after another question.

"Why did Uncle Drayton buy the slave children gifts?" he said to Charlotte, rather too loudly.

Uncle Drayton himself turned. "If my slaves don't want for anything, they won't steal from me," he said. "And it costs me only a few coppers." He looked at Henry-James. "Come into my library—you and your grandpappy. I have instructions for you both."

As it turned out, Austin and Charlotte didn't get to see Henry-James or Daddy Elias again until that night— although they did listen from under the stairs while Uncle Drayton told Henry-James about shining his boots and packing his clothes and reviewed for Daddy Elias that he was responsible for making sure the slaves got to work on time and completed their tasks. The white overseer he'd hired was only there to keep the slaves from taking too many liberties, he told him.

When the children finally did get to go out to Slave Street, it was nearly dark. Daddy Elias was on the porch of the tiny cabin Henry-James shared with him and Ria. Jefferson, now relatively odor-free, crawled right up into the old man's lap. The wrinkled face curved into its spoon-shaped smile, and his breath whistled happily.

"Just what I wanted," he said. "The mos' important people on the plantation, right here on my porch."

"*You're* the most important person on the plantation now, Daddy Elias," Austin said.

"Now, that ain't true, Massa Austin," Daddy Elias said, ducking his snowy-white head.

"Yes, it is! I bet if you weren't a slave, you'd get paid a lot of money for all the important work you're going to do this summer."

Daddy Elias shifted Jefferson on his lap. "I don't know 'bout none of that," he said. "Ain't never had no money. Wouldn't know what to do with it if I had it."

"I know what I'd do!" Jefferson said. "I'd buy me a pin like that one Austin has."

"Now, what pin would that be?" Daddy Elias said.

Austin couldn't keep a smile from spreading all over his face. "I got this from my father today," he said. He took off the pin and held it out so Daddy Elias could see.

"Mmmm-mmmm, that's mighty fine," Daddy Elias said. "Nothin' purtier than the flag of the U.S. of A., less'n it's Miss Lottie's face."

"Why he send you a flag, Massa Austin?" Henry-James said.

"It's to remind me of what he's fighting for," Austin said. "For us to be a united country."

"Austin!" Charlotte said suddenly. "That's what my daddy wants, too. We heard him say that today."

Austin felt the shadows cross his mind again. *The only difference,* he wanted to say, *is that my father believes everybody in it should be treated equally. Your daddy doesn't.*

"Let me see it," Jefferson said. He snatched the pin from

Austin's hand and furrowed his chubby brow over it.

"Hey, give that back, shrimp," Austin said. "Father sent it to *me*."

Jefferson plunked the pin back into Austin's palm and scowled. "How come he didn't send *me* one?" He folded his arms sulkily across his chest.

"Because you would probably lose it," Austin said, replacing the pin on his collar. "And I think this is worth a lot of money."

Daddy Elias rubbed Jefferson's shoulder with a crusty hand. "I think that there pin is worth a lot more than money, Massa Austin," he said. "Now Marse Jesus, He didn't set no store by no gold pins—no, sir."

"What did He set store by?" Jefferson said. He crept back into Daddy Elias's lap.

"Our friend Jesus, He gather things like the freedom and the fair way of treatin' every human bein'—just like that flag stand for. That's what He gather to Hisself. I bet He never own no pin."

"Well, I *do* own one," Austin said.

He pulled in his chin so he could see the pin on his collar. It shone on his shirt even in the dimness of the evening, and it made his father seem close.

His friends around him seemed close, too. Beyond them, the slaves crooned "We are climbing Jacob's ladder" to the stars while the frogs pumped their bass in the background. The scent of roasted pork and apple pies from supper still hung in the air right along with the hot smells of mud and rice water. It was all close and familiar.

"This is one of those picture-perfect moments," Austin said suddenly.

"What you talkin' 'bout, Massa Austin?" Henry-James said.

"Like that photographer said—it's a picture-perfect moment. I wish I could take a picture of *this* moment, because everything is perfect."

"I think them moments happen when we feels the Lord Jesus with us," Daddy Elias said.

"Then Jesus is definitely here," Austin said. "Right this very minute."

But as always, the minute *lasted* only for a minute.

Charlotte squirmed on the step. "Are you going to keep wearing that pin, Austin, even though Daddy said not to?"

"He isn't my father," Austin said stubbornly.

"What would you do with a big old pile of money, Charlotte?" Jefferson cut in.

She looked away from the porch. "I would build another plantation just like this in Flat Rock so I wouldn't have to be away from here all summer."

"I don't want to go at all!" Austin said. "It's better now that Henry-James is going to be with us, but what about Daddy Elias?"

"I ain't never been no place but Canaan Grove," Daddy Elias said. "I think old Daddy Elias belong right here."

"Who's gonna tell us Jesus stories?" Jefferson said, sitting straight up on Daddy Elias's brittle knees.

"I reckon all you young'uns can do that for yourselves," Daddy Elias said. He rested his old eyes softly on Austin. "And if'n you always thinks of Jesus first, before anything else, you gon' be all right. Yes, sir."

"You better tell us a story now, though," Jefferson said, nodding his tousled head firmly. "Just in case."

As Daddy Elias cleared his throat and Henry-James

scooted in closer for the story, Charlotte sidled up to Austin.

"It's going to be a summer without any troubles now," she whispered. "I wish you wouldn't make Mama mad with that pin."

She turned her head then and focused on Daddy Elias. Austin took the pin off and held it in his palm.

Father said to wear it, he thought miserably. *But how can I do it and not make everybody else mad? Why can't things ever stay right for more than a minute?* He curled his fingers around the pin. *I wish Father were here. He'd make Uncle Drayton let me wear this.*

He toyed with his collar—and then he had an idea. As Daddy Elias lit up the porch with his story, Austin lifted his collar, and he pinned the flag to its underneath side.

Chapter Four

They were headed back toward the Big House when Bogie suddenly stopped and quivered his nose up in the air.

"Shhh!" Henry-James hissed at once. "Bogie smells somethin', and it ain't good."

Charlotte edged closer to Henry-James, Austin craned his neck to see around him, and Jefferson craned beside him. He knew Henry-James saw what he did, coming out of the trees. He felt his black friend go as rigid as a post.

"What is it?" Charlotte whispered.

"Oh, Lordy, Miss Lottie," Henry-James whispered back. "It's the Patty Rollers."

From out of the shadows at the end of the long row of pottery and carpentry and tanning shops, two figures stepped, dark against the sunset sky. One was thin, and his beard stood out in a wiry silhouette. The other had shoulders like a bull.

"Run, Henry-James!" Charlotte whispered in a voice so high it squeaked.

"He doesn't have to run," Austin hissed. "He's not off the plantation."

Henry-James's eyes were wide. "That don't matter to them none."

He zigzagged off through the trees. As he did, the howl that pierced the air froze the rest of them in their tracks.

"Bogie, hush up!" Austin hissed.

But Bogie lowered his big head and drove like a cannonball toward the two men, snarling all the way. The wiry man with the scrawny beard flattened himself against the weaver's shop.

"Irvin, it's that there killer dog!" he cried in a whiny voice.

"Call him off, you miserable little cuffee!" Irvin Ullmann said.

Austin could almost see the words grinding out like gravel through his ugly yellow teeth.

Bogie continued to leap and rear up and snarl at the two men. Although he growled back, even bulky Irvin Ullmann kept his distance as he shouted, "Call your smelly dog off, ya cuffee. Get him back, or I'll whip the tar out of you when I catch you!"

"There are no 'cuffees' here," Austin called to the Patty Rollers over Bogie's carrying-on. "Just my brother, Miss Ravenal, and me."

Bogie gave one last bark for good measure and backed away from the men. His tail batted a warning, and drool fell like a shoelace all the way from his mouth to the ground.

Irvin Ullmann stepped from the shadows. Barnabas Brown only peeked out timidly.

"Where'd that darky go?" Ullmann said.

"What darky?" Austin said. "I told you, it's just my

brother, Miss Ravenal and me. You remember me—Mr. Ravenal's favorite nephew."

Austin could feel Charlotte clinging close behind him. His own heart was racing, but he kept his voice calm. He could usually out-talk the Patty Rollers.

Irvin Ullmann moved close enough for Austin to see his bloodshot eyes and yellowing teeth. He and Bogie were both growling under their breath.

"You're lyin' to me, boy. I know better than to trust a Yankee." Irvin spat on the ground.

"Really, Mr. Ullmann," Austin said. "There is a young lady present."

"Not as far as I'm concerned!" Irvin snarled. "As long as she takes up for you, she's no better than a Yankee herself. She deserves whatever she sees."

"I'll be sure to pass that along to her father," Austin said.

"He will, too," Jefferson put in, sticking out his lower lip for good measure.

Barnabas bolted out from the weaver's shop wall. "Mr. Ravenal ain't gonna like that, Irvin," he whined.

"Shut up!" Irvin said. He moved in even closer to Austin—so close that Austin could smell the pork fat on his breath. "You talk big, boy, but like most Yankees, you ain't got the guts to back it up. But I'll tell you one thing you *can* pass along to your uncle."

"Oh?" Austin said. He tried to make his voice sound disinterested. "What's that?"

"Tell him this ain't gonna be a good summer if he don't change his tune. The slaves got their Patty Rollers. Mr. Ravenal, he got his Fire Eaters—and they're gonna burn him up."

He gave one final spit and jerked his head at Barnabas.

They stalked off, and Austin let out a long breath.

He was about to say "Let's go" when two more figures took shape out in front of them, near the stable. There was no mistaking who they were. Austin stopped short, and Charlotte and Jefferson plowed into the back of him.

"What's the matter?" she whispered.

"Polly and Tot!"

Charlotte moaned.

"Quick, where can we hide? I don't feel like getting a Polly lecture."

"This way!" Charlotte hissed.

She yanked him and Jefferson into the stand of trees Henry-James had disappeared into, just as Polly and Tot stepped away from the stables. Behind him, Austin heard Bogie baying playfully.

"Miz Polly!" Tot shrieked. "That dog gonna bite my head clean off!"

Austin cringed as he and Jefferson followed Charlotte off into the trees. Tot had a voice like a fingernail being scraped down a pane of glass.

"Get back, animal!" he heard Polly bark.

Bogie barked back, and Lottie turned around to grin at Austin.

"He'll hold them there for a while," Austin said. "Good old Bogie."

They emerged into a clearing just then, and Austin realized where they were. Rounded stones and wooden crosses poked up from the ground, and the air smelled sweetly of the bunch of honeysuckle someone had put on a grave.

"Isn't this the slave cemetery?" Austin asked.

"Why?" Lottie said slyly. "Are you scared?"

"Of course not!"

"Me neither!" Jefferson said.

"Well, you should be!" said another voice. "You never know who you're going to find here!"

Austin thought he would jump out of his skin. Charlotte grabbed his wrist, and then she started to giggle.

"Kady!" she said.

"I knew it was her," Jefferson said.

Austin let out a puff of air—trying not to act too relieved—and grinned. "What are you doing here?" he said.

"Probably not the same thing you are." Kady stood up from where she'd been sitting at the base of a magnolia tree. She dusted off the back of her skirt with a book she was holding and poked a fat pencil into the knot of dark brown hair at the back of her head.

Austin eyed the pencil curiously. "So what *are* you doing out here?" he asked again.

"It was the only place I could think of where no one else would come. I couldn't stand to hear another sentence about packing. I've been writing some poetry."

Austin wrinkled his nose. "Poetry?"

"I see you're not impressed," Kady said.

"I've always thought poetry was kind of sappy," Austin said. "No offense meant, of course."

"None taken," Kady said dryly. "Although if you want to talk about sappy, listen to Mama and Polly discussing their gowns for hours on end."

Charlotte giggled. "They talk about every last bit of lace."

Kady rolled her eyes. "I get so bored that my *toenails* fall asleep. It'll be good to go to the mountains and get away from all this madness for a while."

Charlotte nodded. "At least in Flat Rock we don't have to worry about Patty Rollers."

But what about the Fire Eaters? Austin thought. The idea poked at him. No more picture-perfect moments tonight.

Kady tucked her book neatly under one arm and held out the other one to Austin. "It's getting too dark to see out here now. Why don't you all escort me back to the Big House before Mama sends a search party to look for me?"

"I think she already did," Austin said. He took her arm and tried to shake off the poking feeling. "We almost ran into Polly and Tot. That's how we ended up here."

"I'm surprised Polly left her hatboxes long enough to look for me." She stopped and tilted her head toward something.

Austin heard it, too. It sounded like someone was breathing very hard.

And as they came around the next tombstone, they saw who it was.

"Henry-James!" Jefferson cried.

Charlotte squatted down to where the black boy was crouched against the flaking picket fence. Austin could see from his friend's expression that he was scared.

And he's almost never scared! Austin thought.

"What happened, Henry-James?" Kady said. "Are you hurt?"

He shook his head as if he were numb.

"Oh," Lottie said suddenly.

"What?" Austin said.

"Yeah, what?" Jefferson said.

"It's nothing. Come on, Henry-James. I'll walk you out."

"But what's going on?" Austin said. "I just want to know."

"And I just want you to hush up!" Charlotte said.

Austin stared as she took Henry-James's elbow gently and helped him to his feet. Charlotte got angry less often than Henry-James got scared. It was one of the few things that *could* hush Austin up.

As soon as they were outside the slave cemetery, Henry-James let out a big puff of air and straightened his stocky shoulders.

"I reckon I better get on home," he said.

"Now what was that all about?" Austin said as the sound of Henry-James's barefoot steps disappeared in the direction of Slave Street.

Charlotte rolled her eyes. "For someone so smart, Austin Hutchinson, you certainly are *stupid* sometimes. Don't you remember? Henry-James is afraid of cemeteries."

"Oh," Jefferson said.

"I should have guessed that," Kady said. "With all the strange stories they tell each other, most of the slaves are. You can barely get them to come in here for a burial!"

Austin folded his arms awkwardly over his chest. "Sorry," he said. "I wasn't thinking straight." Then he called into the darkness, "I won't forget again, Henry-James! I promise!"

As he lay in bed later, Austin tried to imagine the rest of the summer.

Usually he was good at that, but tonight it was hard. In the first place, it was hard to imagine being without Daddy Elias the whole summer. He always knew what to tell Austin when he was in trouble.

But it's supposed to be a summer without troubles,

Austin thought. *That's what Uncle Drayton said.*

He rolled over on his side to catch some of the breeze blowing through the open window.

It'll be hard without Daddy Elias. But what had he said earlier—think of Jesus first?

Austin wasn't sure how to do that. The only thing he could think of was to pray, so he shut his eyes tight.

"Jesus, friend," he whispered. "Could You help me make this a summer with no trouble?" He sighed into the pillow. "I'd sure like a summer of picture-perfect moments."

here was still an early morning mist hanging over the rice fields and a ribbon of pale pink at the bottom of the sky the next day as they got ready to leave Canaan Grove for the train station. They would take the train as far as Greenville and then board a private hack Uncle Drayton had arranged to take them on to Flat Rock, North Carolina.

"I've barely had time to put myself together," Polly whined as she gathered up her crinolines to board the carriage.

"She looks the same as usual to me," Austin muttered to Henry-James.

"I think she looks better," he whispered back.

"Henry-James!" Uncle Drayton called out sharply. "You don't have time to be chewing the fat with Austin! Come help Isaac figure out how to get all these trunks in this wagon!"

Henry-James hurried off with a jolt to one of the two wagons that were already piled high with trunks, bags, and

43

hatboxes. Bogie followed on Henry-James's heels and jumped up into the wagon. Everything on him drooped.

Austin looked at Kady, who was just coming down the front steps. "Bogie gets to come with us, doesn't he?" he said.

Kady cocked her head at him. "I'm sorry, Austin," she said. "I scrubbed him with mud and vinegar until I thought I'd scrape all his fur off, but he still smells like he slept with that skunk for a week."

"I don't smell him," Austin said.

"Well, you aren't Olivia Ravenal," Kady said. "She told me first thing this morning that under no circumstances was that 'mutt' to go to Flat Rock with us."

"Bogie isn't a mutt!" Austin said. "He's family!"

"Maybe *your* family," Polly said behind him. She backed up to get another run at the carriage door, knocking him sideways with her petticoats.

Austin moved sullenly over to the pair of chestnut bays hitched to the carriage and gingerly patted one's nose while he watched Bogie plunk his muzzle on the side of the wagon and follow Henry-James with his agonized eyes.

"Why did you have to wear so many crinolines today?" Kady said.

"Why is that any of your concern?" Polly said as once more she tried to squeeze in the carriage door.

"Because I'm the one who is going to be crushed in a corner by the miserable things," Kady said.

Polly bunched her petticoats up under one arm and took a run at the carriage. The crinolines sprang loose and bounced her backward.

Austin plastered his hand over his mouth, but a large guffaw slipped out anyway—loud enough to startle the horses. They stepped nervously forward, and the carriage rolled slightly with them. Polly's scream ripped the air.

"What on earth?" Uncle Drayton cried.

"My gown—it's caught in the wheel!"

Her shrieks were frightening the horses, and they continued to mince timidly forward.

"Rein in those horses!" Uncle Drayton shouted.

But before Austin could even think about climbing up into the driver's seat, a black body was suddenly there. Henry-James grabbed the reins and pulled them back, shouting "Whoa!" at the nervous team of horses. They stopped, tossing their manes and rolling their eyes until the whites showed.

"My precious baby!" Austin heard Aunt Olivia cry as she rushed with a rustle of silk down the front steps of the Big House.

"Are you hurt?" Uncle Drayton said.

Polly, it seemed, could only wail—and Tot with her. They were both trying to paw their way out of a smothering pile of petticoats.

"Boy!" a voice snapped. Aunt Olivia was looking up at Henry-James, both of her chins crimson and shaking furiously. "What were you thinking of, driving these horses on when the girl hadn't even boarded yet?"

"I's sorry, missus," Henry-James said stiffly.

"Sorry?" Austin said. "You don't have anything to be sorry about!" He whipped his head toward Aunt Olivia. "If he hadn't jumped up there and *stopped* the horses, Polly would have been dragged clear to Flat Rock!"

Aunt Olivia's large brown eyes went into slits. "Then it was you. I might have known."

"No, Mama," Kady said. "It was Polly herself. She was

carrying on so, trying to get these ridiculous crinolines into the carriage, that she spooked the horses and set them off."

"I did no such thing!" Polly shrieked. "If Henry-James had been up there in the first place—"

"You mean, instead of trying to load all of *your* belongings onto the wagon?" Kady said.

"And yours!"

"I put all my things in one trunk, remember?" Kady said.

"Kady!" Aunt Olivia cried. "I told you to pack more!"

"What do I need for sitting under a tree with a book, Mama?" Kady said.

"Sitting under—? Book—?"

Aunt Olivia was sputtering so that once again Austin had to put his hand over his mouth to keep from splattering out a laugh. He could see Charlotte, behind Kady, stifling giggles over her mother's reaction. Her golden eyes were dancing.

"Yes," Kady said calmly. "I intend to catch up on my reading while we're gone. I've been so busy teaching the slave children recently, I haven't had time to tend to my own studies—"

"This is *your* doing, Sally Hutchinson!" Aunt Olivia said. Her voice reached a fever pitch as she whirled to face Austin's mother, who was descending the steps holding Jefferson by the hand.

"Have I missed something?" Mother said. She smiled her soft smile at her sister-in-law, but Olivia was miles from a smile of her own.

"You certainly haven't missed an opportunity to infect my daughter with your ideas of what a woman should be!" Aunt Olivia said. "I was well on my way to transforming Kady into an elegant southern lady when you arrived."

Just then Polly screamed anew.

"What is it now?" Kady said.

"My gown is torn! Look, it's ruined!" She stomped to the front of the coach, hands on skinny waist, and glared up at Henry-James. "Why couldn't you stop those horses sooner, you wretched little cuffee!"

"Don't call him a cuffee!" Charlotte burst out.

"Henry-James didn't do anything wrong, Polly!" Austin shouted.

"Don't you speak to my daughter in that tone!" said Aunt Olivia.

"I will tend to my own son, thank you," Mother said.

"If you tended to your own son, we wouldn't have half the problems we have around here—"

"Quiet, all of you! Before I go completely mad!"

That command from Uncle Drayton halted the shouting. Austin bit at his lip and watched his uncle, who stabbed a finger at the stagecoach.

"Inside, all of you. I am tired of listening to this caterwauling."

"Drayton—"

"Now!"

His trumpet voice blared so loudly that the horses shied. There was a sullen silence as the Ravenals climbed into the coach.

"Massa Austin," Henry-James whispered as he climbed down from the coach to take his place on a wagon with Tot, "I don't think just bein' away from them Patty Rollers is gon' make this a summer without troubles like Miss Lottie said."

Austin sighed heavily as he followed his mother, Jefferson, and Ria into the carriage. He stopped on the step and looked back over Canaan Grove. The slaves were just now making their way about to do their tasks, and Austin's heart skittered a little as he spotted Daddy Elias among them, his old frosty head bent against the morning heat.

Austin knew he himself must look like Bogie did as he watched the old man.

Please come with us, Daddy Elias! Austin wanted to cry out to him. *Things are falling apart already, and we haven't even left the plantation yet.*

He knew what Daddy Elias would say, of course. *"You young'uns gon' be all right. You just think 'bout Jesus before anything else."*

"All right, Jesus," Austin whispered. "Please take hold of this summer. It's already gotten away from the rest of us."

But things didn't get any better when they arrived at the train station. The conductor complained to Uncle Drayton as Henry-James and Isaac made 20 trips from the wagons to the baggage car—with Bogie following his master's every step—that they had far too much baggage. He also warned Uncle Drayton that there were no dogs allowed on the train.

Aunt Olivia screamed when a shower of ashes and cinders rained down on them from the locomotive's smokestack and burned a hole in her gown. She also bellowed when she saw Bogie and said he'd better be put on the wagon back to Canaan Grove with Isaac.

And when Henry-James ordered Bogie to stay in the wagon while he made his last trip, Bogie threw his big head back and howled from the pit of his soul. Austin could barely stand to see him in such pain.

But once Uncle Drayton shooed them all aboard the train, Austin forgot about all of that.

In all of his 11 years of riding on trains back and forth across the northern United States, Austin had never seen anything like the car they stepped into. He had always sat on a hard-backed seat facing his parents in *their* hard-backed seats, with dozens of other weary, complaining, and sometimes stinky travelers packed in around them. This couldn't have been less like that.

"Good heavens, Drayton, a private car?" Austin's mother said.

"We never travel in anything but a Pullman," said Aunt Olivia as she floated across the carpeted floor to a plush sofa with dangling gold fringe.

"This particular one is called 'The Countess'," Uncle Drayton said proudly.

It certainly looks as if a countess could live here, Austin thought.

The wooden ceiling was elaborately carved and polished to a high shine, and the windows were all hung with pale blue velvet drapes that were tied back with gold braid. There were enough gold and blue brocade sofas and overstuffed chairs for all of the Ravenals and Hutchinsons, plus Tot, Mousie, Henry-James, Ria, and Josephine. That is, if any of them could sit instead of looking into the gold-rimmed mirrors or exploring the sideboard that groaned with refreshments.

"If you could have traveled like this with Wesley, I doubt you'd have fallen so ill," Uncle Drayton said to Sally Hutchinson as he escorted her to a chair opposite Aunt Olivia's sofa. "Unfortunately, it costs $50 a day, and I don't think Wesley makes that kind of money giving lectures and writing pamphlets."

"He doesn't work to make a lot of money," Mother said coolly.

"Obviously," Aunt Olivia said. She raised her eyebrows at Mother's gray frock.

Charlotte tossed her stuffed rabbit onto a chair and tugged at Austin's sleeve. "Let's go explore the rest of the train," she whispered.

That did take his mind off the bristly feeling that was creeping under his skin. The South Carolina Canal and Railroad Company's train was something to see. The steam locomotive, with its tall smokestack shaped like a funnel, was called "The Phoenix." Behind it there were the usual passenger cars, and then the ladies' car, where the women could ride in comfort and escape the smoking and spitting of the male passengers. The men had their own car, too, with seats running all around the edges and a table in the middle, covered with newspapers. Even the sleeping cars were more luxurious than the ones Austin had seen in the North. They had curtained berths, all cushioned and cozy. Austin wanted to crawl into one and test it out, but Charlotte begged him not to.

"How long will it take us to get to Flat Rock?" Austin said as they felt the train lurch forward and begin to creep along its track.

"We'll get there tomorrow. We'll stop at an inn tonight and refreshment saloons during the day, although we have our own food in our car."

"Let's go have some," Austin said. "Maybe the arguing will be over by now."

Charlotte headed off through the sleeping car toward the Pullman, which was at the end of the train. Austin followed, until he heard something from inside a berth that made him stop—and listen.

"Ravenal's aboard," a man's voice said. "I saw him get on with his family."

"They were late, then," said another. "I was afraid they'd missed the train. Your man is ready in Greenville?"

"Don't worry about a thing, Ches. It's all set. We'll get Ravenal. Don't you worry. We'll get him."

Chapter Six

ike a cat on a fence rail, Austin crept away from the curtained berth and caught up with Charlotte. She had already jumped the few feet onto the platform of the Pullman car, and Austin followed clumsily.

"Does your father know anybody named Ches?" he said, huffing for air.

But she put her finger to her lips and nodded toward the Pullman car. From inside, words were being batted back and forth like a ball.

Charlotte rolled her eyes. "They're at it again. At least maybe they won't notice us dipping into the snacks, they're so busy arguing."

Austin followed her in, his face now hot with nervousness.

"We'll get him," the man had said. And he'd mentioned Uncle Drayton's name.

What did they mean, they'd get him? Austin thought. *Should I tell Uncle Drayton?*

But he couldn't have broken into the conversation

anyway. It burst out like a blast from the smokestack the minute they opened the door. Aunt Olivia's was the first voice he heard.

"We are not on board a half hour and already the conductor has had to pay us a call! I am mortified, Drayton!"

"It's not as if we've been accused of derailing the train, Mama," Kady said.

Austin could tell Kady was having a hard time keeping back a smile. His mother wasn't even trying. She was grinning from one earlobe to the other.

"It is all the same as far as I am concerned," Aunt Olivia cried. "I told you this boy was not fit to be your valet!"

Austin snapped his head toward Henry-James, who was stuffed between a chair and the wall.

"Boy!" Uncle Drayton trumpeted out. "Did I not tell you no less than three times that your mutt was not to be allowed on this train?"

"Yessir, Marse Drayton," Henry-James said. His voice was strong, but he was speaking carefully.

"Then you deliberately disobeyed my order and stowed him aboard the baggage car anyway."

Austin felt his eyes bulging. Bogie was aboard the train!

"No, sir, Marse Drayton, I did not," Henry-James said.

"Oh! The impudence!" Aunt Olivia cried.

"Then how is it," Uncle Drayton said, shushing her with a wave of his hand, "that he is now sleeping amid our trunks like a paying passenger?"

"I don't know, Marse Drayton," Henry-James said. "I just knows Bogie, he's powerful smart. If'n he wants to do somethin', he gonna find hisself a way."

Kady couldn't contain herself any longer. She let out a guffaw that rivaled any of Austin's and doubled over in her chair, with Austin's mother hooting just as loudly beside her.

"I fail to see the humor!" Aunt Olivia said. "It will be all over the train before we reach Columbia that the Drayton Ravenals have sneaked a dog aboard—and not one of Drayton's prize hounds, but some mangy mongrel."

"I wouldn't be quite so concerned about that," Sally Hutchinson managed to say between chuckles. "I'd be more worried about the fact that said mongrel is right now about to enter this car!"

They all looked toward the door. Bogie had his paws up on the window and was peering in, while the conductor was fumbling with the handle with one hand and holding a handkerchief over his nose and mouth with the other. The door flew open, bringing in with it an earful of racket and a noseful of track dust—and a handful of Bogie. In spite of the rope that was tied around his neck, Bogie charged across The Countess toward Henry-James, knocking over water decanters and umbrella stands on the way.

But it was the noseful of fading skunk odor that drove them all squealing for their hankies. Austin ducked behind a chair with Charlotte, coughing and laughing until he could barely breathe.

"If you insist on traveling with this animal," the conductor shouted above the fray, "then you'll have to travel with him in here!"

With that, he slammed the door, and Bogie joined in the shouting with a howl of his own. Uncle Drayton shut them all up with a bugling, "Quiet!"

Austin peeked out from behind the chair. Mother and Kady were still choking back laughter. Aunt Olivia had swooned and was being revived by Ria, Mousie, and

Josephine. And Polly and Tot were both standing on a sofa, shrieking and clinging to each other. Only Bogie looked content as he dropped his bag-of-bones self at Henry-James's feet, sighed, and closed his eyes. Jefferson darted over to him and hugged him around the neck.

"You're brave, little man," Uncle Drayton said. Austin was relieved to hear a hint of a smile in his voice. "That is one of the foulest odors I have ever smelled."

"Jefferson doesn't care," Kady said, wiping her eyes. "He smells the same way, just not nearly as strong!"

"Drayton!" Aunt Olivia cried as she pulled herself up from the couch. "I cannot abide this! I am going to the ladies' car!"

It took all of the ladies except Mother and Kady to get her there. When she was gone, Sally Hutchinson sank back against the tufted chair and chortled again.

"You are more extravagant than I thought, brother," she said to Uncle Drayton. "Fifty dollars a day for a private car— for your dog!"

To Austin's utter amazement, Uncle Drayton threw his head back and roared out a laugh so long and hard that he had to sit down.

"Just keep that animal away from my wife, boy," he managed to say to Henry-James as he slapped his knee. "Or both you *and* the dog will find yourselves beside those railroad tracks with the alligators!"

And then he laughed again until the steam whistle screamed them to a stop at St. George.

"Why don't you children go and get yourselves an ice?" he said. Still chuckling, he flipped a silvery quarter to Austin. "And I'll go see if I can make amends with Olivia."

By the time the children had all hugged Bogie and had

their ice cream while sitting on the train depot railing swinging their legs, Aunt Olivia and Polly and their "court" had been lured back into the Pullman, and Polly was ready with a bottle of rose water she'd brought along.

Kady doused Bogie with it. Henry-James muttered under his breath that now Bogie smelled like a sissy dog, but Bogie himself seemed quite pleased. He couldn't stop sniffing himself as he flopped down at Polly's feet. She recoiled and squealed until Henry-James dragged him off into a corner—far away from Aunt Olivia.

For a while there was a pouty silence. That gave everyone plenty of time to store up their complaints about how much sweat was trickling down their middles and how ineffective Mousie, Tot, and Josephine were at keeping them cool with their peafowl fans.

Austin tried to concentrate on the swamps and marshes they passed, hoping to see a cottonmouth snake hanging from a cypress tree or an alligator sunning himself on a bank.

But once they left the low country behind, the terrain grew boring, and when he tried to read a book, the words vibrated in front of him with every clatter of the train's wheels. By the time Polly finally broke the silence, Austin had a few gripes of his own that were ready to pop from him.

"Why can't Tot and I have a couch together?" Polly whined. "Aunt Sally and her slave girl are sharing one."

Kady wriggled impatiently. "Because you're already taking up enough room for two people."

"Besides, Ria isn't my slave girl," Austin's mother said firmly. "She's my nurse."

"A fine job she's doing, too," Aunt Olivia said. "You're looking so much better, Sally, no one would ever guess you'd been sick at all. And Flat Rock is such a healthy place, by the time you finish a summer there, you'll be as fit as the rest of us. You'll want to go back north with Wesley—"

"Olivia!" Uncle Drayton said sharply.

There was silence again. It lasted until Austin thought he'd crawl out of his skin—and then Mother said, "Ria, what about one of those wonderful spooky stories you used to tell us? I think we need one of those now."

"I don' know, Miz Sally," Ria said. She darted her eyes uncertainly at Aunt Olivia.

Austin brought his cheek out of his hand and sat up with interest.

"She did have some wild ones—I remember that now!" Uncle Drayton said. "Tell one, Ria. Wasn't there something about a cane and a graveyard?"

Austin felt a delicious chill. "Tell it, Ria! That sounds good!"

Aunt Olivia sniffed and turned away, but Uncle Drayton settled back in his chair and said, "Go on, Ria. Scare us half to death the way you used to."

Ria sat up straight in her seat and closed her eyes for a minute. When she opened them, they were bright and hard with the story behind them.

"It happen a good while back," she said in a voice as foreboding as fog. "Some gentlemens and ladies, they was having theyselves a party—fancy party, you know—with the ladies all in dresses wider than the door."

"The way Polly wears them," Kady said.

"Hush up, Kady," Polly said.

"And there was a full moon out that night as the gentlemens took the ladies out on the porch for to look at the stars—only the clouds, they was rushin' in and nobody couldn't hardly see the moon. It set all the ladies to shiverin'—all excep'n Miz Nellie."

"What did Miss Nellie do?" Mother said, though Austin was sure she knew full well.

"Oh, Miz Nellie, she just throw her head back and laugh, and she say she ain't scared of no night—nohow." Ria's eyes narrowed. "And one of them gentlemens—who wasn't no gentleman at all, 'scuse me for sayin'—he say, 'Even if'n you was in a graveyard, you wouldn't be scared of the dark?' And Miz Nellie, she say, 'No, sirree. You send me out into any old cemetery and I just laugh at that old moon.' "

"No!" Polly cried. "They didn't send her out to the graveyard!"

"Yes'm, they did," Ria said, nodding her head solemnly. "She jus' laugh in they faces and head for the door. Only one gentleman, he say, 'You better take this here cane of mine, Miz Nellie, just in case.' So Miz Nellie, she laugh again and she take that ol' cane and she go on off to the graveyard."

There was a pause as Ria gathered herself up and leaned forward. Everyone else leaned with her. Even Aunt Olivia turned her face in Ria's direction.

"Now Miz Nellie, she jus' march her sweet self right down the street to that there graveyard, and she step right up to the grave of the meanest, most miserable ol' man what ever lived, and she laugh up at the moon and she wave that ol' cane in the air and she shout, 'I ain't afraid o' nothin', nor nobody!' And then she brung that ol' cane down to the groun'—and then somethin'—somethin' jus' come over Miz Nellie."

Ria stopped.

"Well, for heaven's sake, what?" Aunt Olivia said. "What came over the girl?"

Austin poked Charlotte. Lottie didn't respond. She was clutching the toy rabbit and listening, wide-eyed.

"She didn't know what it was her own self, missus," Ria said. "All she know is that she can't move, not a muscle. She frozen, right there in that there graveyard. She can't run, she can't walk, she can't do nothin' but just stand there a-starin' at that grave. And all she know is that all of a sudden, she scared—so scared, she die of fright right there."

"Oh, no!" Polly said.

"Oh, yes'm," Ria said with a sage nod. "Them gentle-mens what sent her out there, they finds her the nex' mornin', stiffer'n a board." She paused and looked at them all with her eyes gleaming. "With that there cane stuck in her skirt, holdin' her right there to the ground."

"What?" Kady said. "You mean the only thing holding her to the ground was that cane that she'd poked into her skirt?"

"That's right," Ria said.

Aunt Olivia grabbed Mousie's arm and fanned herself frantically. "Oh, thank heaven!" she said. "I didn't know what to think!"

"My, my, Ria," Uncle Drayton said with a grin on his handsome face, "you haven't lost your touch. You can still tell a mighty fine story."

"I like Daddy Elias's Jesus stories better," Jefferson said, scowling. "They aren't scary."

No, Austin thought. *But that sure put everybody in a better mood.* And it was a mood that lasted for the rest of the day, and even the next—until they reached Greenville.

There was a big, black, shiny stagecoach with the words "Greenville Line" painted on its side in fancy gold letters waiting for them at the train station to take them to their hotel. Two covered farm wagons followed in the dust, piled high with their trunks and bags and boxes—and Bogie.

"My heavenly days, Drayton," Sally Hutchinson said when they lighted from the coach at the hotel. "I thought the inn we stayed in last night in Columbia was lovely, but look at this splendid place."

"Certainly you didn't expect anything less," Aunt Olivia said as she brushed past her.

"Certainly not," Mother murmured.

"'The Mansion House'," Austin read on the sign.

It was definitely the most elegant inn the *Hutchinsons* had ever stayed in, what with its curlicued trim on the outside and its heart pine floors and circular stairs on the inside. Aunt Olivia was already whining to Polly that the Colemans who owned the hotel had the Louis XV French Victorian furniture she'd been begging Drayton to buy her for nearly a year.

"Look," Austin said to Charlotte. "The parlor is so big they have to have two fireplaces."

"And wait until you see the bed chambers," she said. "Come on!"

She started up the stairs, hauling her rabbit, with Austin behind her.

"Don't you dare take that dog up to any of them!" Aunt Olivia hissed to them—and then her face suddenly sprang into a wreath of smiles. "Why, Susan Pryor!" she oozed. "How wonderful to see you!"

Austin watched from the stairs as Aunt Olivia stretched out her plump, jeweled hands to a blonde woman in Spanish lace who floated toward her with her wide skirts rocking.

Oh, brother, Austin thought. *They're going to coo over each other like a pair of turtledoves. I'm getting out of here.*

But as he turned to head up the stairs to join Charlotte, the blonde woman answered in a voice so cold it even froze Austin to the steps.

"Hello, Olivia," she said.

There was an awkward pause. Austin sneaked a backward glance at Aunt Olivia. She was fanning herself anxiously and blinking at Susan Pryor.

"Will you be at supper?" Aunt Olivia said.

"Yes," said Susan. She pulled her lace shawl up over her shoulders and gave a frigid smile. "But our table is already full."

She started to pass, but Aunt Olivia pawed at her arm. "Then we'll see you in Flat Rock. I'm giving a tea on—"

"I have plans," Susan Pryor said, and she sailed off to the other end of the parlor to join three other well-dressed ladies who smiled woodenly at Aunt Olivia and began at once to whisper among themselves.

Aunt Olivia stared at them for a moment before she gathered her traveling dress primly into her hands and moved toward the stairs, blinking as if she had something large and bothersome in each eye.

Austin hurried on up the steps. And for the first time ever, he felt sorry for his aunt.

✠ ◆ ✠

Chapter Seven

Supper that night was an elegant affair, and Aunt Olivia presided over the Ravenal table as if she were entertaining Governor Pickens. Austin noticed that she kept glancing at the other tables where Susan Pryor and her friends sat whispering behind their fans. Every time they laughed, Aunt Olivia took to giggling, too—like she was having the time of her life. Only her eyes gave her away. They always darted back to the Pryors' table, looking envious and hurt.

"I always thought Aunt Olivia and Uncle Drayton were popular in Charleston," Austin had said to his mother up in their room when they were dressing for supper.

"They always were," she'd said, "until Uncle Drayton started thinking for himself. Whenever something is important to you but isn't important to the crowd, you're going to find yourself losing friends."

They sure don't act like her friends, Austin thought now as he watched the women appear to stab her in the back with their knifed gazes.

But it was easy to forget about that after supper. Then the inn turned from an elegant dinner house into a beehive of activities. There were six tables for playing whist on the side porch and three card tables set up in the parlor. Someone played the piano and several of the ladies gathered around it to sing, while in the men's sitting room, billiard balls popped against each other amid outbursts of masculine laughter.

A crowd of young people headed for the spring, dodging the pairs who were pitching quoits on the lawn.

"Dancing begins in the ballroom at nine o'clock!" Mr. Coleman called after them.

Uncle Drayton settled himself on the front porch with Henry-James stationed behind his chair and Mother and Aunt Olivia sitting on either side of him. From the lawn where he and Charlotte and Jefferson sat eating watermelon, Austin could see how self-conscious Aunt Olivia looked as the other ladies breezed past her, laughing and talking together.

"Do you see, Drayton?" she said to her husband. "Do you see what you've done? Even Adolpha Rhett won't speak to me! She was my best friend in Flat Rock last summer!" She sniffled. "There is nothing worse than feeling like an outsider."

"Good evening, Mr. Ravenal," someone said.

"Who's that?" Austin whispered to Charlotte as he watched a pointy-nosed man with long hair approach Uncle Drayton on the porch.

"Roger Pryor," Charlotte whispered back. She giggled. "Watch what he does with his hair."

The two men shook hands, and Uncle Drayton offered

him a seat. Aunt Olivia looked as if she'd pop open with joy when he accepted.

"You're headed for Flat Rock?" Uncle Drayton asked.

"I am," said Mr. Pryor. His voice seemed to come directly out of his nose. "It's always good for my health up there in the mountains, though I can't say it will be the same for yours."

"What on earth do you mean, Mr. Pryor?" Aunt Olivia said, flattening her hand to her chest.

With a birdlike jerk of his head, Roger Pryor tossed his hair aside. Charlotte gave Austin a poke, and he grinned.

"I'll get right to the point," Mr. Pryor said. "Your friends are unhappy with you, Ravenal. I'm afraid they're going to make your summer in Flat Rock most uncomfortable if you don't make a better showing of your loyalty."

"My loyalty is right where it has always been," Uncle Drayton said, voice as smooth as honey. "To the United States of America."

"Even though that same United States has turned against the great state of South Carolina?" the man said. The hair got another toss.

Uncle Drayton's voice turned to molasses. "I see no one turning against South Carolina, Roger. Least of all me."

"Really? Then why is it that you no longer support slavery in the South?"

"I do not support *secession*, Roger. There is a difference."

Roger Pryor tossed his hair again, first in one direction and then the other. "There is no difference! We must secede if we are not allowed to continue to own slaves. There is nothing else for the South to do."

"Only because the slave owners control the South!"

Austin's chin fell to his chest. It was his mother talking!

"And they make up one fourth of the population—the *white* population, that is."

"Now Sally," Uncle Drayton said. His voice was back to honey and thinning fast. "That is because we slave owners are respected men."

"Oh, yes, I know," Austin's mother said. "I was raised down here, remember? The more human beings a man holds by force against their will, the more respected he is!"

"You are not talking about just any human beings, ma'am," Roger Pryor said. "We are talking about Negroes."

Mother's face went blank. "So?"

"So . . . we have proven in our years of raising them that they need to be taken care of."

"Taken care of?" Mother said. "Because they are not capable of taking care of themselves? Is that what you're saying?"

"I'm afraid I have to agree, sweet potato pie," Uncle Drayton said. He had one restraining hand on Aunt Olivia's arm and the other on Mother's. "I mean, it's quite obvious. Henry-James, step out here!"

Uncle Drayton snapped his fingers in the air, and Henry-James stepped quickly from behind the chair. Austin put down his watermelon rind as Uncle Drayton took the black boy by the arm and gave him a shake.

"Speak, boy," his uncle said.

Austin nearly spoke himself. Henry-James's eyes went woodenly to the porch floor, and his lips twitched in fits and starts.

"Speak!"

"I ain't got nothin' to say, Marse Drayton," Henry-James said.

Austin twitched as if he'd been jabbed.

"You see?" Uncle Drayton said. "They can't think for themselves."

Roger Pryor nodded. "That's right."

"What do you expect?" Mother said. She slapped her hands down on her knees. "Until a few months ago, you refused to educate them!"

Mr. Pryor tossed his hair indignantly, and Uncle Drayton let go of Henry-James and waved him off as if he were an annoying fly. "I have never met a slave yet who was capable of deep thought or anything but surface affection for another person."

"That's because you don't trouble yourself to get to know any of your own 'property'!" Sally Hutchinson said fiercely. "They know you want them to be docile and gentle and cheerful in their work, so that's the way they act around you so they won't be punished!"

"And if we did not expect them to behave that way," Roger Pryor said, "they would never do a thing. They hate to work—"

"They hate to do *your* work!"

"They steal!" Aunt Olivia chimed in. "I have to keep all the storerooms locked or the rest of us would starve."

"Slavery seldom fortifies honesty," Mother said.

Aunt Olivia looked confused.

You don't know what fortifies *means*, Austin thought angrily. *Henry-James can think rings around you!*

Austin tried to catch Henry-James's eye, but the black boy was keeping his gaze nailed firmly to the floor.

"Let me put it this way," Uncle Drayton said, lowering his voice to its honey-soft level. "If I were to ask any one of my slaves who knows better what is good for him, he or I, he would say it was I."

"Well, in the first place," Mother cried, "he would be whipped 10 ways to Sunday if he were to say himself! And in the second place, you've tried to suppress their thoughts and fill their minds with your own so they won't have any sense of themselves separate from you."

"Because that's what the good Lord would have me do," Uncle Drayton said.

Mother's mouth fell open. "What?"

"Supreme Court justices, senators, famous writers—they've all said that God intends for the Negroes to be slaves."

Mother leaned back in her chair with such force that Austin thought for a moment she had fainted. Ria moved quickly toward her, but Mother shook her head at her. "What happened to the man who was going to think for himself now?" she said.

"It sounds like that's all changed!" Aunt Olivia said gaily. "Thank you, Mr. Pryor, for clearing that up!"

"No," Uncle Drayton said. "I am thinking for myself when it comes to politics. But who am I to question what God says?"

"I have never heard God say that! Where in the Bible does Jesus say that any person is less than another?" Austin's mother sat forward again, and although her cheeks were flushed, her voice was strong. "You are just looking for a way to make it acceptable to keep slaves so you can also keep your luxurious way of life, Drayton Ravenal. You are too good a man to actually believe the things you have said here."

"The woman is talking nonsense, Ravenal," Roger Pryor

said. "I haven't time for that. I want to know where you stand on secession."

Uncle Drayton gave his sister one last long look before he answered. "I think it is far too drastic a measure," he said finally. "There are other ways to settle the matter. If we separate ourselves from the rest of the nation, it will be like sitting on a branch while we saw it off from the tree. There will be war."

"You'll be fighting a war of your own in Flat Rock, then!" Roger Pryor cried through his thin nostrils as he leaped from his chair. "Rhett and myself—we're traveling all over North Carolina this summer preaching the secession word. We're rallying the people, I tell you. And whoever is not with us is against us!"

"That doesn't frighten me in the least," Uncle Drayton said smoothly.

"Oh, it will, Ravenal," Roger Pryor said. "It will."

Something about his voice made Austin come straight up on his knees. *Where have I heard something like that before?* he asked himself. *Words like that—words that sounded like a threat?*

But before he could think about it further, Roger Pryor turned on his heel and steamed down the steps and across the lawn. Aunt Olivia exploded from her chair and burst toward the front door into the inn. Uncle Drayton sighed and went after her.

"You wants me to come, Marse Drayton?" Henry-James said.

"No!" Uncle Drayton barked and then disappeared inside.

The slave boy's eyes came up off the floor at once, and he charged down the steps and off among the pine trees' long shadows. Austin, Charlotte, and Jefferson took off after him.

They didn't catch up until they were almost to the carriage house and Jefferson called out, "Wait, Henry-James! You're supposed to be looking after me!"

Henry-James stopped then and turned and held his arms out. Jefferson scrambled into them and up onto Henry-James's shoulders.

"Where were you going?" Austin said.

"Jus' walkin'. Walkin' and thinkin'."

Austin gave a bitter snort. "And they said you don't know how to think. Don't believe a single thing Uncle Drayton said about you not being as good as us."

Henry-James looked around cautiously before he answered in a low voice, "I don't. I jus' be tellin' myself what I learned from Daddy 'Lias long time ago: Jesus gather me to Hisself like a treasure, jus' like He do a white boy. I don't got to have nobody tellin' me that. I jus' got to know it in my heart."

Austin stared. "It doesn't bother you when Jefferson has a thousand toys and you have one little wooden dog—or Polly has three trunks full of clothes and you have two old ragged shirts and a pair of trousers?"

Henry-James opened his mouth to answer, but a twig snapped behind them. Austin and Charlotte whirled around, but Henry-James took longer to turn with Jefferson on his shoulders. By the time he did, a man had stepped out of the shadows. All of them—except Jefferson—gasped at once.

He was a tall man with long legs. Even in the almost-dark, they could see his eyebrows tangling over the bridge of his nose like a pair of caterpillars.

Austin recognized him right away, and he could tell from

the stiffness in their backbones that Charlotte and Henry-James did, too. It was Eyebrows Rhett, the mean secessionist from Charleston.

But Rhett didn't seem to recognize them. "What are you children doing out here?" he said gruffly. "The party is inside."

"I was gon' see to my massa's horses," Henry-James said in a clear voice.

"You watch your tone with me, boy!" Eyebrows Rhett said.

What tone? Austin thought. *He was just answering your question!*

But he'd come up against the secessionists before. These weren't men to be argued with.

"Now all of you, back to the inn—before I tell your parents!" Mr. Rhett barked.

They bolted for the Mansion House.

"Who *are* your parents, anyway?" he shouted after them.

But no one answered. None of them even looked back, except for Austin, briefly. When he did, his foot caught on a root that stretched up from the ground at the base of an oak. He sprawled on the grass and squeezed his eyes shut tight.

He'll be after me any second now! he thought. *Then he'll recognize me for sure, and there will be even* more *trouble!*

He lay still for a moment, waiting, while his friends' footsteps faded into the music that jangled from the inn.

"All clear now, Mr. Rhett?" a hoarse voice whispered behind him.

"Yes! Mr. Chesnut gave you your instructions?"

"Yessir!"

"Then see that you follow them to the letter. And report back to me when you're through."

"Where is Mr. Chesnut?"

"He stayed in Columbia. You take your orders from me now. It's all the same. We're all in this together."

"Yessir," the hoarse voice answered.

"If you do a decent job, I'll keep you on—and your brother, too."

"What about my sister?"

"We'll talk about her later. Go on now. Get it done."

There was one more "yessir" before Austin heard footsteps again. He cringed into the grass, waiting for a rough hand to pluck him up by the back of the shirt, the way it had done once before.

But neither set of feet passed him, and it was suddenly silent . . . except for the faint padding of feet heading away, toward the carriage house.

Cautiously, Austin lifted his head and looked around. There was no tall, mean Mr. Rhett. There was only the shadowy figure of a lanky, big-boned boy disappearing into the carriage house.

Without really knowing why, Austin scrambled up from the grass and followed.

It was probably none of my business, he told himself as he crept to the doorway of the carriage house. *It's just that I kept waiting for them to mention Uncle Drayton's name.*

But his thoughts were strangled by what he saw.

The lanky boy with the hoarse voice was sliding beneath a coach . . . the coach with "Greenville Line" painted on the side in gold letters.

✠ ⚜ ✠

ustin took a step forward, the words *Hey, what are
you doing there?* teetering on his lips. But before
he could get them out, something flashed past him
and sent him flying against the wall. A howl ripped through
the air.

There was a bumping sound from under the coach.

"Ouch!" the hoarse voice spat out. "What is *that?*"

As if in answer, the howling got louder. Bogie slid across
the carriage house and under the coach. Austin scrambled
out the door and watched through a crack as the big-boned
boy kicked and contorted and finally got himself out from
under the coach with Bogie snarling, drooling, and snapping at his calves. The dog chased the boy all the way out
of the carriage house and across the stable yard.

Austin stayed put until the baying stopped and Bogie returned, snuffling and snarling. He lifted his black nose into
the air and sniffed.

"It's just me, Bogie," Austin said. "Good job!"

Bogie seemed to shrug his baggy shoulders modestly

72

and then licked Austin's palms.

"I don't know what that big ox was doing under our coach," Austin said. "But you stand guard and don't let him come back, all right?"

Bogie nuzzled his hand.

Later, Austin flopped like a trout from one side to the other on the hotel bed. Snatches of overheard words and flashes of threatening faces made a mess in his mind.

Pointy-nosed Roger Pryor tossing his long, greasy hair—*"I'm afraid they're going to make your summer in Flat Rock most uncomfortable."*

Tall, mean Mr. Rhett with his caterpillar eyebrows—*"Mr. Chesnut gave you your instructions. Go on now. Get it done."*

Pryor talking through his nose—*"Whoever is not with us is against us."*

Another voice hissing behind a sleeping car curtain—*"Don't worry about a thing, Ches. It's all set. We'll get Ravenal."*

Did the boy under the coach have anything to do with all that? Austin wondered. Was Uncle Drayton really in trouble?

And then he felt the poking feeling again. *After the way he treated Henry-James on the porch tonight, do I even care whether he is or not?*

Austin felt for the flag pin he'd tucked under his pillow and squeezed it tight.

"Austin, my love, you are making me seasick," his mother whispered from her bed across the room. "What's got you tossing and turning so?"

"I wish he were here," Austin whispered back.

He heard his mother stir under her covers, and in the

moonlight he could see her propping herself up on one elbow.

"Who?" she said.

"Father. I guess that's silly."

"If it is, then I'm silly, too," Mother said. "I was just thinking the same thing."

"He doesn't act like Uncle Drayton . . . and I used to think Uncle Drayton was better." Austin squirmed. "But now, I don't know. Sometimes I think Uncle Drayton is the best person in the world—you know, the way he bought the toys for the slave children and let Kady teach the slaves to read and takes care of you and me and Jefferson." He paused only long enough to swallow. "But then he does other things, like the way he made Henry-James stand up in front of everybody while he talked about how he wasn't as good as white people. Father would never do that!"

"They're both good men," she said in a voice as soft as the darkness. "But it's the things they value that make them different. You're beginning to decide what's valuable to you, and that's why you're seeing Uncle Drayton differently now." She sighed. "Don't be too hard on him, Austin. God and I, we're working on him. But we have to give him time."

"I'll try," Austin said, though only half of his heart was in it.

"Try to get some sleep now," she said. "We have a long day tomorrow."

Austin turned over and watched the moon.

What's valuable to me? he thought. *The only valuable thing I own is my flag pin.*

He felt for it under his pillow again and held it tightly in his fist.

It's more valuable than French Victorian furniture and

crinolines, if you ask me—and Uncle Drayton won't even let me wear it.

Let him be in trouble then. Let them "get him." I don't care.

And then he fell into a troubled sleep, the kind that happens when a person doesn't care.

They got ready to set off at dawn the next morning—nobody's best time. While Polly whined that the short night had left ugly bags under her eyes and Aunt Olivia scolded Charlotte because she was "too old to be carrying that ridiculous rabbit around," Austin found Henry-James. He was trying to shove the last hatbox into a wagon. There was a platform for trunks—called a boot—on the back of the stagecoach, but there wasn't nearly enough room on it for all of the Ravenals' things.

Austin found himself gazing across at the stagecoach. It was rounded at the bottom and swung on wide leather straps. He had a sudden urge to climb underneath it—but instead, he asked Henry-James, "Does the coach look all right to you?"

Henry-James gave the stout coach with its four horses only a glance. "It look fine to me, Massa Austin," he said. "I don't know much 'bout stagecoaches. I gots enough to worry 'bout gettin' all this here stuff into this here wagon."

He nodded at the wagon with its bowed frame. Even its cover of sheets couldn't hide the multitude of trunks and boxes that were crammed inside.

"I wish I were riding in here with you," Austin said.

"We'll be trailin' way behind you," Henry-James said. " 'Sides, it's plenty crowded, what with me and Mousie and Tot and Josephine and Bogie."

"Yeah, but I bet you all don't argue about your crinolines the entire time."

Henry-James's lips twitched. "No, I reckon we don't. Why you ask me 'bout that stagecoach, Massa Austin?"

"Maybe I'm just being stupid—" Austin leaned in closer "—but last night, I saw somebody, a boy—"

"Henry-James!" Ria called from the direction of the coach. "Get this here dog out of this stagecoach before missus find him, or he gon' be a *dead* dog!"

Henry-James took the yard in three steps and dragged Bogie out. Then the big-bellied driver climbed up onto his high seat and blew his long tin horn to announce that they were leaving. There was no time to tell Henry-James about the boy under the coach.

Besides, it seemed sturdy enough when all nine of them climbed aboard and each took their 15 inches of seat on three benches. Austin was scrunched into the middle bench with Charlotte and the rabbit, Jefferson, and Kady.

"This is brand-new," Mother said from her place between Ria and Polly in the front.

"The whole line is new," Uncle Drayton said. "All private coaches. They'll travel to suit the passenger."

"Can they travel without bumps?" Aunt Olivia said. "This is the worst part of the trip with all that wretched jostling around over those awful mountain roads."

"That's the fun part," Charlotte whispered to Austin. "Just wait."

As they set off up State Road toward Saluda Gap, where the Buncombe Turnpike would take them to Flat Rock, Uncle Drayton stared out the window of the back seat as if his mind were even farther away than the 36 miles to Flat Rock. Aunt Olivia spent a lot of time sniveling into her handkerchief. But Sally Hutchinson seemed determined to have a good time.

"Now, everyone knows to spit out the leeward side of the coach, right?" she said gaily.

"How rude!" Polly cried from the front bench.

Kady nudged Austin and grinned.

"No," Mother said. "Rude is when you lop over on your neighbor when sleeping. Or point out places on the road where horrible murders have been committed."

"Actually," Kady said, eyes dancing, "the worst thing you can do is grease your hair before you start out."

Polly blinked back at her. "Why?"

"Because enough dust will stick in it to grow potatoes."

"Why must you people be so crude?" Polly said. And she turned around and sat with her arms folded across her chest for the next hour.

Austin busied himself looking out the window. At first all he saw was row upon row of corn and wheat. The lines whipping by began to hypnotize him, and between that and the steady rattling of the coach and the occasional snapping of the whip, his eyes drifted closed.

Some time later, a large pothole opened them. As the coach-and-four tossed everyone about, Austin gasped.

"What's the matter, Boston?" Charlotte said.

Austin could only point out the window.

"Haven't you ever seen mountains before?" she said. "Those are the Blue Ridge."

Austin could see why they were called that. Before him, gentle peaks rolled under the sky and reflected its blue. To Austin, it looked as if the earth had been gathered up and shaped by God's hands like soft clay. Plump and lush, the hills folded one into the next in tree-covered piles.

Everyone talks about how beautiful Uncle Drayton's house and Aunt Olivia's gowns are. He took a big breath. *But this—this is* really *beautiful.*

From then on, it didn't matter how much sweat stuck his hair to the sides of his face or how much road dust flew into his eyes or even how much Polly whined. The mountains were all he could think about.

"I'm tired of riding!" Jefferson complained. He tried to spit, but his mouth was too dry. "Where are we going, anyway?"

"Right up there to those mountains," Kady said. "In the highlands beyond the mountain crest."

"And we're actually going to live *there*, right *in* the mountains, for the *whole* summer?" Austin asked.

"I told you," Charlotte said with a poke.

After a few stops to water the horses and pay tolls, at noon they reached the foot of Saluda Mountain, just before the state line between North and South Carolina, and the stagecoach driver gave a blast on his tin horn. The folks at Hodges Place, a half inn and half farmhouse, were ready with dinner on the table.

But food was the last thing on Austin's mind. He ran across the dell to stare at the mountains without the tiny stagecoach window restricting his view. It was another picture-perfect moment, he decided.

"You really like those mountains, don't you, Boston?" Charlotte said at his elbow.

"They're incredible! Has Henry-James ever seen them?"

"No, he's always stayed behind at Canaan Grove before—"

"Then let's find him and see how he likes them!"

Austin grabbed Charlotte's wrist, but she shook her

deer-colored head at him. "We won't see Henry-James for a while. That covered wagon can't travel as fast as the stage-coach."

"He's probably just passing through Traveler's Rest," Kady said, coming up beside them. "But don't worry, you'll have plenty of time to look at the mountains with him when we get to Flat Rock."

Austin shrugged. That would have to do, then.

Kady nudged him softly. "I think you have a poet's soul, Austin Hutchinson," she said.

"Poet's?" he said. He wrinkled his nose. "Not me!"

"Anyone who gets that excited about sharing a mountain view with a friend is a poet down deep, that's for sure," she said.

After downing okra stew and biscuits and gravy, they were off again. Even after paying another toll of seventy-five cents, Uncle Drayton was in a better mood than he had been that morning.

Probably because that Colonel Hodges and his wife were nice to him, Austin thought.

"It's worth it to pay the extra money for a fine, private coach," he said as they began a serpentine crawl up the steep mountain. "This buggy hasn't given us a bit of trouble."

"Maybe not you," Aunt Olivia said. "I'm nothing but bruises after all this bouncing around."

Charlotte and Kady rolled their eyes at each other, but Austin looked contentedly out the window. He had been silly to lose sleep wondering about the boy under the coach last night. If he'd done anything to hurt the coach, they'd have known it by now. Bogie was a good guard dog.

It was easy to forget all that, too, as the road wound through the thick forests with their deep-green hollows.

Now and then he spotted a waterfall. Sometimes for miles at a stretch there was nothing but flowers, all in the colors of flame. Then for a while he'd lose count of the trees— weeping willows and such, some of them covered with grape-heavy vines that connected the branches to each other.

At one point, the grade was so steep that the stagecoach rocked to a stop and the big-bellied driver told them all to get out and walk for a bit as he let the horses pick their way to safer ground. Austin couldn't contain himself any longer. He raced ahead of everyone and got to the crest, where he could see all the way to the misty blue horizon.

"We're at the top!" he shouted.

Aunt Olivia stopped, causing Mousie to plow into the back of her, and threw her hands over her eyes. "I can't bear it!" she cried. "I'm always so frightened here, Drayton!"

"Why?" Austin said. "The road is at least 17 feet wide. Even if the horses decided to run away with the coach, there's very little chance of our tumbling over the side before the driver got control."

"Thank you, Austin," Uncle Drayton said quickly, as Aunt Olivia began fanning herself in a frenzy. "I'm sure we all feel much safer now."

Austin shrugged and looked around. "What's that stone slab there?"

"That's the marker," Kady said. "You're now in North Carolina."

"The worst of it is over now, Olivia," Uncle Drayton said as they moved toward the coach again. "As I recall, the road goes down the other side of the mountain gradually, and we'll have all those lovely hedges you like to look at. Once we've gone beyond Saluda Gap, we're practically there. It's downhill all the way."

"And downhill is the hardest on my team," the driver grumbled. "So if we could all climb aboard, Mr. Ravenal?"

Austin was the first one in, scrambling for his place at the window.

"Excited, Austin?" Kady said mildly.

Austin nodded and poked his whole head out.

"Next bump we go over, you're going to be sorry you did that," Polly said.

"Let him find out for himself—if he's so smart," Austin heard Aunt Olivia mutter.

But even that didn't curb his excitement. He did pull his head in, but he clung to the window frame with both hands.

"I want to see!" Jefferson said as he tried to squeeze in beside him.

Austin moved over an inch, never taking his eyes off the mountainside as they galloped at what seemed like full tilt down the slope.

"Mother!" Jefferson wailed. "Austin won't let me see out!"

"We're coming to a bridge!" Austin called out to him. "I'll let you see when we get closer."

And they were getting closer—fast. The stone-lined bridge lay below them at a sharp curve in the road, and the stagecoach was barreling toward it at breakneck speed.

"Whoa, now!" the driver shouted above the pounding of hooves on the dirt road.

But none of the four horses seemed to be paying attention, and the coach swayed crazily to the left, dumping Austin squarely on top of Jefferson—and Charlotte and Kady, too. There was a chorus of squeals as the coach righted itself, and Austin clawed his way back to the window.

The only thing he saw as he poked his head through the opening was the right wall of the bridge coming up toward them.

"We're going to crash!" Austin cried.

The horses veered sharply to the left and missed the wall.

But the stagecoach sailed off to the right as if it had wings—and dove straight for the creek below.

Chapter Nine

With a slam, the bottom of the coach hit the creek bank. Austin clung to the window frame and watched one wheel and then another fly past. And then he saw nothing as the coach turned on its side and slid. Austin couldn't turn his head—there was something heavy on top of him. It crushed him down until the coach finally crashed to a tilted halt.

For a moment there was silence except for the rushing of the creek somewhere below them. Austin opened his eyes, but all he could see was a mass of petticoats.

I'm alive, though, he thought. He tried to move his hand to be sure the rest of his body was all there, but his arm was trapped somehow.

"Is everyone all right?" he said, though his voice only squeezed out through his mouth, squished against the side of the coach.

"I'm dying!" Aunt Olivia cried. "Has everyone else been killed?"

"No, Mama," Kady said. Something on top of Austin

moved. "I'm all right, I think. Lottie, honey?"

"Something is squashing me, but I think I'm all right," Charlotte said.

"That's me squashing you," Kady said. "And we're both squashing Austin."

"What about me?" said an angry little Jefferson-voice. "I'm a pancake!"

"I'm dying!" Aunt Olivia cried again.

"What is it, Livvy?" Sally Hutchinson said. "Where do you hurt?"

"Everywhere! I'm dying!"

"Where's my hat?" someone else called out.

"Polly's all right," Kady said. "What about you, Aunt Sally?"

There was a faint giggle from the front seat. "I'm perfectly fine, thanks to Polly's crinolines. I'll never complain about your petticoats again, my love!"

"You sure you all right, Miz Sally?" Ria said.

"I'm perfectly fine, but if you can, you'd better get back there and check on Olivia."

Aunt Olivia was still squawking like a terrified chicken, but Ria couldn't move to get to her—and neither could anyone else. After a few moments, it was apparent that they were trapped inside their capsized coach.

"Can you reach the door, Kady?" Mother called over Aunt Olivia's screeching.

"No," Kady said. "It's up near my feet."

"Try kicking it," Austin said.

She did, but the door wouldn't budge, and the coach slid another few inches. There was a new round of screaming.

"Is anyone out there?" Kady shouted.

Nothing.

"The driver must be hurt badly," Austin said.

"Not half as badly as I am!" Aunt Olivia cried. "Get me out of here!"

"Perhaps Drayton can kick the door open," Mother said.

And then there was a stricken silence. For the first time, Austin realized they hadn't heard a word out of Uncle Drayton since they'd crashed.

"Daddy?" Kady said. "Daddy, are you all right?"

"Drayton!" Aunt Olivia screamed.

If he didn't hear that, he isn't going to hear anything, Austin thought.

He wriggled and squirmed—with Charlotte saying, "Ouch, Austin, don't!"—until he could see over the middle seat. Behind him, there was a mass of silk and petticoat lace. From under it, he saw the top of a deer-colored head. A thin trail of blood trickled down from it.

"He's hurt," Austin said. "I see blood."

Aunt Olivia squawked anew, and Polly, too, began to cry loudly.

"How much blood, Massa Austin?" Ria said.

"Not that much," Austin said. "About as wide as a piece of yarn, coming from the top of his head."

"It don't sound so bad, Miz 'Livia," Ria said.

"What do you know?" Aunt Olivia sobbed. "He's dying. I know he is!"

"Mama, for heaven's sake, hush up!" Kady said.

"Try to get his head up into yo' lap, Miz 'Livia," Ria said.

"I can't move. I'm dying, too!"

"Wait!" Austin said suddenly. "Everyone quiet!"

"Don't you tell me to hush up—I'm hurt!" Aunt Olivia said.

"No, I hear something. Somebody's coming!"

There was a hopeful silence in the coach. Sure enough, the heavy clopping of farm horses' hooves resounded through the woods. Austin squeezed his eyes shut to hear better, and he caught the creaking of a wagon, too.

Even as they listened, there was a familiar howl. The hoofbeats slowed, and then quickened. There was shouting and rattling, and the wagon came to a halt. Bushes crashed and twigs snapped as someone, whimpering and panting, charged down the embankment.

"I think that's Bogie!" Charlotte said.

And then someone screamed "Miz Polly!" as if she were scraping all of her fingernails down a tin pail.

"Tot!" Polly screamed back. "Come save us. We're all dying!"

"Good Lordy, they's dying!" said a full, rich voice.

"No, Josephine!" Kady called out to her. "We're all fine except Mama and Daddy."

Bogie, in the meantime, was barking and baying as if he were beside himself.

"I knows they's in there, Bogie," said another voice. "Everybody gon' be all right, Miz Kady. You jus' hang on and don't move around none."

"Henry-James!" Austin said.

"Why shouldn't we move?" Mother called out. She had to shout over Aunt Olivia's wailing and Bogie's howling.

"'Cause if'n you does, this here coach gon' go crashin' right into that there creek," Henry-James said. "You jus' hold on 'til I brace it with somethin'."

"I can't hold on!" Aunt Olivia cried. "I'm dying, Drayton's dying—"

"Oh, shut up, Olivia!" Mother snapped at her.

And there was silence, except for Charlotte's soft,

slightly hysterical giggling in Austin's ear.

It seemed like forever before anything happened outside the coach. And then they heard grunting and groaning and Henry-James saying, "Jus' a little farther now. Good. We gon' set it right here."

There was a loud thud near the front of the coach.

"What was that?" Aunt Olivia said timidly.

"We done put a log in front of the coach so you can't slide none, missus," Henry-James said. "Now we can try to get this here door to open."

Once more, there were sounds of grunting and Henry-James giving instructions.

"It's caught. Mousie, you hol' on to me, and Tot, you grab her. Josephine, you be pullin' all of us. And Bogie, you get yo' jaws on Josephine's skirt. That's it."

And with a crack, the stagecoach door came open above them and promptly fell off onto the ground. The first person to the opening was Aunt Olivia.

"Get out of my way, darky!" she cried. "I have to get out!"

"I thought she was dying," Mother muttered.

"I ain't never seen a more 'live woman in my life," Ria muttered back.

After a mad rustling of Aunt Olivia's silk, Henry-James said, "You can grab hol' of my hand, Miz Kady."

One by one they were helped from the coach by Henry-James. But when Kady, Charlotte, and Jefferson were peeled off Austin, he couldn't bring himself to get out. He climbed over the seat and looked down at Uncle Drayton.

He was gray and his eyes were closed, but Austin could see his breath stirring the ruffles on his shirt. The blood trickled down into his neatly trimmed beard and disappeared. A large lump of guilt formed in Austin's throat.

"My Drayton is dying!" Aunt Olivia was wailing outside. "Someone help him!"

Ria crawled back into the coach and dabbed at the wound on Uncle Drayton's head with her apron.

"How Marse Drayton doin'?" Henry-James said from the opening.

"He gon' be all right. You go tend to that driver, Henry-James. Get some water from the creek for his head and don't move him. His leg's broke."

She looked at Austin as Henry-James left the coach. "You wanna help me with Marse Drayton?"

Austin nodded, and he could feel his eyes filling up.

"He gon' be all right," she said. "Ain't no need for cryin'."

Outside the coach, they could hear Aunt Olivia screaming. "Boy, why are you helping that idiot driver? It's his fault we crashed in the first place!"

"No," Austin said in a low voice. "It was my fault."

Ria only stared at him for a few seconds before she nodded and said, "Then you better help him get well. Go on and get some water on a cloth and some rags for bandages, too."

Austin crawled out of the coach, fighting back the tears. *It is my fault! I should have told somebody about the boy under the coach. I should have!*

"What are you doing?" Charlotte said from behind him as he stumbled down toward the creek.

"I have to help Uncle Drayton!" Austin said.

Charlotte's eyes sprang open with alarm. "I thought Ria said he was going to be all right."

Austin could only swallow. He took off his shirt and drenched it with the cool, clear water that raced over the rocks in the creek bed, then dashed back to the coach. As he climbed in, Charlotte ripped her petticoat into strips and handed them to him one by one from the stagecoach doorway as Ria bathed Uncle Drayton's face and wrapped his head.

"He just need some of that good mountain air now," Ria said. "Tell Henry-James to pull him on out of here. You all make a bed on the groun'."

Kady donated her petticoat for a pallet, and to Austin's surprise, Polly pulled off enough of her crinolines to rival any featherbed Austin had ever slept in. Aunt Olivia knelt by Uncle Drayton's side as Henry-James and Josephine stretched him out on the makeshift bed. She looked a little shamefaced, Austin thought.

But not even close to how ashamed I feel.

He knelt down on the other side, and he tried to pray.

Jesus, I'm sorry. I thought I was putting You first, but it got messed up somehow. Help us, and please, don't let him die.

There was quiet all around them. The sun splashed through the trees here and there. Below them, the water tumbled over its rocks and into the arch beneath the bridge that looked like a church door. The only other sound was Jefferson whispering to his mother, "That water running makes me have to use the necessary!"

Ria got down on her knees beside Austin and began to talk and sing in one smooth murmur. "Lord Jesus," she crooned. "Please let this sweet air fill Marse Drayton. Let it open his eyes and carry him back to us, sweet Jesus."

Austin closed his wet eyes and nodded. "What she said, Jesus, friend," he whispered. "Please."

There was a soft moan.

Before Austin could get his eyes open, Aunt Olivia was screeching like a hoot owl.

"Drayton, you're alive! Oh, thank heaven! Drayton!"

"Certainly I'm alive, darlin'," he said in a weak voice that sounded nothing like his usual trumpet. "I'm far too ornery to die."

There was enough hugging and kissing and crying then to sweeten an entire pot of mush. Thinking his own thank-yous, Austin squirmed out of the group. He was shaky with relief, but the guilty lump was still firmly lodged in his throat. His head wouldn't stop pounding out thoughts.

It was still my fault. I should have told somebody about that boy and what I overheard the men saying.

That boy must have done something to the wagon. He must have after all.

But how could he with Bogie there?

Maybe it wasn't my fault—maybe the driver really was an idiot, like Aunt Olivia said.

There was only one way to find out.

He found the stagecoach driver with Henry-James, who was propping his head up on the cushion from the driver's seat, and Bogie, who was attempting to lick the man's forehead.

"Get this animal away from me," the man grumbled. "He smells funny."

Bogie took the hint. He picked up something from the ground and trotted off with it. Austin vaguely recognized it as Charlotte's rabbit, but he had other things on his mind.

"I s'pose you got a hundred questions," Henry-James said to Austin.

"Just one," Austin said.

Henry-James grinned down at the driver. "Now that there is a miracle."

But Austin couldn't grin. "What happened?" he said to the man.

"That's what I'd like to know," the man growled. "One minute I'm driving down the road pretty as you please, and the next minute, I can't control the horses. It was like the reins weren't connected anymore! And then, the whole thing broke loose and the horses went one way and we went the other. Next thing I knew I was thrown clear to—"

"What do you mean it 'broke loose'?" Austin asked.

"Just what I said!" the driver roared. "Something was bad wrong with those straps. They only held until we started downhill!" He winced and grabbed his leg. "I want a doctor."

"My mama, she's good as any doctor," Henry-James said. "And here she come now."

Austin got up and stumbled toward the bridge. Charlotte and Bogie found him there, hanging over the stone wall.

"Bogie found Rabbit!" Charlotte said. "He must have gotten thrown from the stagecoach!"

Austin grunted.

Charlotte looked at him closely. "I thought you were mad at my daddy," she said, "but you aren't acting like it."

Austin rubbed his eyes to squash down tears. "I was—I am. I don't know!"

Bogie whined and lay down against the wall.

"You're confusing me," Charlotte said.

"I'm confusing myself!" he said. "First I'm mad at him because he makes a fool of Henry-James, so I don't care that somebody's trying to hurt him. Then when he does get hurt, I hate myself. I can't get it all figured out!"

She didn't point out that tears were now pouring down

his face. He was grateful for that. She only said, "But you can *always* figure everything out, Boston."

"Not this time," Austin said miserably.

They were both quiet for a while as they watched the water swirl and fall and disappear under the bridge. Austin swallowed the lump in his throat and wiped the tears with the back of his hand. After a while, Charlotte began to giggle.

"What?" Austin said.

"Did you know you were standing out here in your . . . 'linens'?"

Austin looked down at his undershirt. "You mean, my 'unmentionables'?"

Charlotte gave another soft chortle. "Do you dare me to say 'underwear'?"

"Double dare you," Austin said. He couldn't help it. He could feel a smile teasing at the corners of his mouth.

"Underwear," she whispered.

"Charlotte Anne Ravenal!" Austin said in his best Aunt Olivia screech. "Genteel people do not speak such a word aloud!"

"Underwear!" she whispered again. And then she took off across the bridge with Austin hauling after her. The rushing of the water was joined by their gales of too-long-bottled-up laughter. Austin wriggled his shoulders as he laughed, just to shake off the poking he could still feel.

Henry-James was sent off on one of the wagon horses to get help. It was nearly dark before two more covered wagons pulled up and the Hutchinsons and Ravenals and their slaves were piled on board one and the stagecoach driver was placed in the other.

Austin could hardly keep from laughing at the spectacle

Polly made, piling into the wagon, haughtily holding on to the silk-flowered poke bonnet that she had retrieved from under Mother's feet in the stagecoach. He hoped no one would tell her there was a footprint on the brim.

Aunt Olivia herself refused to get in.

"I am absolutely mortified at the thought of riding in a farm wagon, Drayton!" she said. "I would prefer to wait for another stagecoach."

"Not from the Greenville Line," Uncle Drayton said, as Henry-James and Josephine lifted him into the wagon. "A coach would have to be in shabby condition to fall apart the way this one apparently did."

Austin looked hard at the ground.

"Then another company!" Aunt Olivia cried. "Not a covered wagon!"

But Uncle Drayton murmured something about purchasing that Louis XV French Victorian furniture, and with a sigh she climbed aboard.

Austin sat beside Henry-James on the driver's seat of the wagon that carried the trunks as they made their way on to the North Carolina side of Saluda Gap, where Uncle Drayton said there was an inn they could stay in. Austin was glad to be away from Aunt Olivia's screeching voice, but he didn't have much to say himself.

"You got somethin' eatin' away at your tongue, Massa Austin?" Henry-James said.

"No. Why?"

"'Cause you awful quiet. You had a few things to say to that there stagecoach driver."

Austin shrugged, but he could feel the lump returning to his throat, bigger than before.

"I had me a look at the coach just now, like you asked

me about 'fore we lef' Greenville."

Austin looked at him sharply. "What did you see?"

Henry-James shook his head. "Jus' like that driver say— them straps done broke. Only . . ."

"Only what?" Austin said.

"Only it look like they been notched with a knife."

"But I don't understand!" Austin cried. "I thought Bogie was guarding the coach!"

Henry-James looked at him sideways. "Guardin' the coach? How he s'pose to guard a coach when he locked up in a horse stall all night with a big ol' bone to chew on?"

"What?" Austin said.

"That's where I foun' him this mornin'. He done cleaned the meat clear off'n that bone, too."

Austin put his hands on his knees and buried his face in his palms.

"Don't you worry 'bout it none," Henry-James said. "Miss Lottie, she keep tellin' me this gon' be a summer without no troubles, and 'spite of myself, I's startin' to believe her."

"How can you say that?" Austin said into his hands. "We just had a coach wreck—that I could have prevented."

"But jus' looka here, Massa Austin," Henry-James said. He gave Austin's elbow a nudge. "You ever seen anything like this in yo' life before?"

Austin brought his head up and looked out over the scene Henry-James was pointing to. The sun was setting behind the mountains, leaving only the last of its fiery flames above the dark, sleepy treetops.

"It feel different up here, don't it, Massa Austin?" Henry-James said.

It did. The air was light, and the ground didn't seem to

be alive with critters. There wasn't the racket of locusts, birds, and frogs. There was a peace about it—a crystal-clear peace.

"You know what I thinks, Massa Austin?" Henry-James said.

"What?"

"I think 'cause we's so high up, we's closer to the Lord up here."

"You do?" Austin said.

"I do—and Massa Austin, I think that do make things different somehow."

Austin thought about it as the last of the sun's flames licked at the tops of the hills.

You're right, Henry-James, he decided firmly to himself. *It* is *going to be different. I'm going to be different. I can't change what already happened, but I'm going to be better now.*

I'm going to be picture perfect.

Chapter Ten

"There's Farmers Hotel!" Charlotte said the next day, peering out the window of the new stagecoach Uncle Drayton had managed to find.

"Even if we aren't welcomed in Flat Rock," Aunt Olivia had said as she'd climbed aboard that morning, "at least we don't have to arrive like a wagonload of poor whites."

"What does she have against poor whites?" Austin had asked.

"They're not rich whites," Kady had told him.

But now Austin was much more interested in what *Charlotte* was saying as she pointed out the Flat Rock landmarks.

"The church is up that way farther," she said, nodding up the main road as they turned off onto a long drive. "There's a graveyard there."

"Can we go?" Austin said.

"Why on earth would you want to go there?" Polly said. "I prefer the parties and the barbecues—"

"If we even get invited to any this year," Kady said.

Aunt Olivia sniffed. "Don't you worry about that! I am going to give a tea party as soon as possible—and we'll just see who snubs Olivia Ravenal in Flat Rock!"

The rest of the conversation faded into the background as Austin hung out the window and watched for the Ravenals' summer house to come into view. They crossed a bridge over a lake so clear and still that it reflected the fir trees around it like a mirror. The coach, with the wagon behind it, climbed a gently sloped hill, and suddenly there it was—a white house sprawling among the firs, pines, and red maples.

"It's not nearly as big and fancy as the house at Canaan Grove," Polly said—as if she were apologizing.

"I like it better!" Austin said.

"For heaven's sake, why?" Polly said.

Austin wasn't sure why. It just looked cheerful and friendly, not grand and proper. There was a welcoming front porch with steps up to it from two sides . . . and a sunroom on one side and another across the front on the second floor . . . and windows and dormers that looked out like neighborly eyes. The front lawn rolled down from it in an endless soft carpet to the lake, and behind it the mountain beckoned him to climb and explore. He squirmed to get out of the coach and get started.

"I want to go everywhere!" he said.

"Well, first you will go upstairs and unpack your things," Aunt Olivia said briskly. "You and your mother and your brother will be in the sunroom in the front."

Austin liked the sound of that—and he liked the look of it even better. After charging past the piece-of-pie-shaped library to the left of the front door and the parlor on the right, both with fireplaces and doors leading to their side porches, he peeked into the ladies' sitting room behind the parlor, the dining room behind that, and the three rooms to the left of the dining room reserved for Aunt Olivia and Uncle Drayton. Then he raced up the narrow, U-shaped staircase behind Charlotte to the next floor.

Four bedrooms opened onto a square hall—one for Charlotte, one for Polly, a third for Kady, and one for a guest room. Between Charlotte's and Kady's rooms, there was a narrow hall leading to a long room that stretched across the front of the house. There were three beds there—and yellow shafts of sunlight pouring in through the windows.

"This is our place!" Jefferson cried, hurling himself to one of the windows and pressing his hands and nose against the glass.

It does feel that way, Austin thought. *It feels like a home for Hutchinsons—more homey than our rooms at Canaan Grove.*

But I wish it were all *the Hutchinsons*, he thought with a sudden shadow. *I'd* really *be happy if Father were here.*

No, I'm going to be different now, he told himself firmly. *I'm not going to sulk. I'm going to put Jesus first like Daddy Elias said.*

"Come on, Austin!" Charlotte called from the hall. "The trunks haven't even been brought up yet for us to unpack, so let's go exploring!"

They rumbled down the steps, leaped over boxes and trunks, and skittered down another set of steps to a cool, dark place with a dirt floor.

"What's this?" Austin asked.

"It's a cellar," Charlotte said. "This is where the slaves will stay—and where we can hide out without anyone seeing us."

She crooked her finger at him, and he followed her to a shorter-than-usual door. She pushed it open and they stepped through it—out behind the house, where the rest of the place called to them like an eager, inviting playmate.

Charlotte took him down to the lake and over the bridge and through a stand of poles-with-leaves.

"What are these?" Austin said.

"Bamboo! We'll make fishing poles out of them!"

"What are those trees? Their leaves look like little fans!"

"Ginkgoes. They're from China. We can climb them and look in Polly's window and scare her!"

"What's up there?" he asked.

"Big Glassy Mountain—a whole thousand feet above all the others. We can play up there—"

Suddenly she stopped, breathing hard, just the way Austin was in the thin mountain air.

"Do you know what, Boston?" she said. "This has never seemed like so much fun before. Now it's all different."

"Why?"

"Because . . . you're here . . . and Jefferson and Henry-James. I was always so lonely here before. I played with Rabbit all the time, and that was all."

She shrugged and smiled a smile that out-dazzled the sun, then took off toward the woods.

"Where are we going?" Austin called after her.

She tossed her hair over her shoulder. "You wanted to see the cemetery, didn't you?"

Shrimp-colored St. John's Chapel sat up on a hill, surrounded like a fortress by a forest-guard of pine and fir trees. It looked like a pretty enough church, but Austin's eyes were drawn right to the graveyard. It was arranged in broad steps that went from the bottom of the hill to the church itself.

Each section was enclosed by a spiked, black railing fence with a gate that swung open at a touch.

Austin hesitated to go in any of them. They were, after all, somebody's family graves. But Charlotte let herself right into one and grinned for Austin to follow.

"I like it in here," she said. "It's . . . cozy."

Austin looked around at the cushiony rug of pine needles on the ground and the tiny pine cones lying here and there. The sun made designs on the gravestones between the shadows, and plush moss grew over everything, giving it a soft look.

"They're like little yards," Austin said.

Charlotte nodded. "That's what I liked to pretend. I used to play house in here when I was little." She pointed to a white marker that reminded Austin of a writing tablet. "I like these thin ones. I used to pretend they were children I could play with. Is that silly?"

"You're supposed to be silly when you're little," Austin said, shrugging generously. "What were these?"

He was looking at a row of rectangular gravestones, raised above the ground.

"I imagined those were old grandfathers sleeping," she said. "That ivy growing around them was their blankets."

Austin glanced around at the row after row of enclosed sections, each on a different level from the others, stretching out like a maze among the shadows.

"We could still play some fun games here," he said. "If you thought it was, you know, all right—being a graveyard and everything."

"Like . . . what kinds of games?" she said.

"There are lots of good hiding places. We could pretend that you were lost in here—had been for days . . ." He could feel his mind warming up to the idea. "And I was sent to search for you."

"Only you have a fear of graveyards," Charlotte added. "You were raised by someone who told you a whole bunch of scary stories."

"It was a black nanny, I think—"

Charlotte's eyes were glowing. "Let's go. You cover your face while I hide, just to make it more real."

I'll do better than that, he decided as she ran off. *I'll go all the way out to the road and walk back up, like I'm discovering this for the first time.*

And so the game was on. Austin tore down the path to the road, turned around, and walked sedately up it again, gazing up at the graveyard with wide, serious eyes and thinking he must look like his father doing that. He stopped once or twice, took a few frightened-looking steps backward for effect, then pretended to force himself forward to the work that had to be done.

By the time he reached the first platform of graves, he had worked up a few actual beads of sweat on his upper lip and was feeling the part.

"Charlotte Anne," he called out quietly. "Are you here? Don't be afraid. It's me—A. T. Hutchinson. I've come to rescue you."

A. T. Hutchinson, that sounds good, he said smugly to himself. *Whenever Mother or Father call me "Austin Thomas" I know that means I'm in trouble. But A. T., that sounds so . . . adult.*

He went on along the path, stones popping under his feet in the silence.

"Charlotte Anne, call out to me and I'll come find you," he said.

But there was no answer. Charlotte Anne, it seemed, was enjoying this part of the game too much to reveal herself yet. Austin let himself into another gated section, this one populated by tall crosses and monuments scattered like statues.

Stepping carefully across the pine needles, he approached one—and darted behind it.

No Charlotte Anne.

He tried the next one, whirling around to make sure she wasn't stealing from one to another behind his back. Holding his breath, he sprang behind still another. A tiny figure in a tattered gingham dress and ragged braids jumped up and stared at him with big hazel eyes—frightened eyes.

And then she gave an almost soundless peep and scampered off like a squirrel.

"Wait!" Austin called after her. "It's all right. I'm not going to hurt you!"

In fact, his heart was racing, probably every bit as fast as hers. He hadn't expected to find another soul besides Charlotte in the graveyard—at least not one that was alive, anyway.

He took a minute to let his heart slow down, and then he resumed his search for the lost "Charlotte Anne." He was a little more careful about springing behind tall gravestones, though. He and Lottie were obviously not the only children who thought this was a good place to play.

Taking hold of one of the black fence spikes, he swung out of that section and followed the path to the next. He peered into it, but he didn't go in. It was filled with all low slabs—no place for Charlotte to hide. The next had several rows of the thin markers, the ones Lottie liked. Austin let himself into that section and ran his hand across the soft moss that grew over the top of the first grave marker.

" 'Eliza Blake,' " he read out loud. " 'Ten years old.' "

Somebody died when she was 10 years old! That's younger than I am!

It was a chilling thought. He took his next step softly, carefully. When he leaned over the next gravestone, the sight of a body lying behind it sent him shivering backward to the gate.

"It's all right, Austin!" Lottie whispered. "It's just me!"

"Oh!" he whispered back. "I knew it was. Really."

There was a soft giggle. Austin straightened his narrow shoulders and marched toward the grave again. He looked down, registered the proper shock and sorrow, and then knelt next to the "body" of Charlotte Anne.

"I didn't expect to find you dead," he said.

"You didn't expect to find yourself dead either, did you, boy?" said a voice behind him. "But that's what's gonna happen to ya!"

This time, Austin nearly jumped out of his skin. He lurched up and backed all the way to the fence. The spikes dug into his behind, but he felt nothing . . . except the horrible hammering of his heart.

Even when he saw that it was just a boy—several inches shorter than himself—it took a minute for him to catch his breath. Charlotte scrambled up from her grave and hurried over to him.

"Well, hello," Austin said to him, attempting a grin. "I didn't know anybody else was playing here. I'm—"

"I know, you're A. T. Hutchinson," the boy said. He tossed his head back in a way that reminded Austin of someone else he'd seen recently. His scraggly, no-particular-color hair flipped away from his face for a moment, revealing a pair of small, snapping black eyes. They made Austin think of the black in a black-eyed pea.

"So, what's your name?" Austin said.

"Izard," the boy said. "Izard Wydell."

Austin felt his lips twitching.

"What's so funny?" the boy said. He left his lips parted at the end of the question, and Austin could see that he was missing several teeth in various places. But from the sharpness of his features, he had to be at least 12. Austin, of course, was curious.

"How did you lose your teeth?" he said. "If you don't mind my asking."

"I do mind!" Izard said. He moved menacingly forward.

Austin felt Charlotte edge closer and grab on to his sleeve.

"And I also mind you scarin' my little sister half to death!" the boy said.

"Oh," Austin said. He showed his own full set of teeth in a big smile. "Was that your sister? I told her I was only playing a game. I didn't mean to scare her."

"Is that why she near to wet her pants after you chased her out?"

"I didn't chase her out!"

"She says you did—and I believe her before I believe any of you rich folks from Charleston, that's for sure!"

Austin wiped that out with a wave of his hand and an even bigger grin. "Oh, you see, I'm not one of those 'rich folks from Charleston'. I'm just here with—"

"Shut up, liar!" Izard shouted. "Before I set my big brother on you!"

"Good grief," Austin said. "How many Wydells *are* there?"

"More than there are Hutchings, I can tell you that."

"Hutchinsons," Austin said.

"I don't care what your name is!" Izard jerked his head back again. "You don't mess with the Wydells. Fergus!"

"And Fergus would be your big brother?" Austin said. He was still trying to sound calm, and he thought he was doing a rather good job—that is, until Fergus appeared at the black gate.

He was lanky and big boned. And in a hoarse voice, he said, "What is it, Izard? Are these young'uns botherin' you?"

Chapter Eleven

All calmness deserted Austin, like a thief running out the door. The gangly boy at the gate was the same boy he'd spotted under the coach.

The coach whose straps had been cut with a knife.

" 'Tain't me they give a hard time to," Izard said. " 'Twas Georgiana."

Fergus came over the fence in one long, lanky step and stood towering over Austin and Charlotte. Austin looked up at him and once again tried to smile.

It was the first time he'd seen the boy close up. He had the beginnings of whiskers poking out on his upper lip and chin, so he was 14 at least—but the "huh" that hung on his big, lazy lips, as if he had just said it or was about to say it, made him look younger than his scrappy little brother.

"What do you want me to do with them?" Fergus said. His mouth stayed open as if he were going to catch Izard's reply like a frog catching a fly.

"What do you mean 'do' with us?" Austin said. "You don't have to *do* anything. We'll just play in our section and you can play in yours."

"That ain't the point!" Izard snapped.

"Oh," Austin said. His heart was starting to pound again. "What is the point, then?"

"The point is you bein' a fancy, rich young'un with nothin' better to do than scare little girls in a graveyard!"

Austin nudged Charlotte with his elbow. "Are you scared, Lottie?"

She nodded stiffly.

"Well, then," Austin said to Fergus, "I guess you don't have anything better to do either—"

"We are workin' people!" Izard cried. His voice was as scraggly as his hair, and the redder his face got, the higher his voice rose, like a piglet squealing.

"What kind of work are you doing in the graveyard?" Austin said. "I don't see any shovels, so I suppose you're not grave diggers."

"We was just passin' through!" Izard said. "We work for Mr. Pryor and Mr. Rhett. Makin' good money, too."

"Congratulations," Austin said. "Why don't we let you get back to it? We'll just be going on home."

"You'll just be goin' wherever I tell you to go, rich boy!"

Austin's heart was pounding now in earnest. And the poking feeling started between his shoulder blades like there was a sword going to work on his backbone.

"You're not our boss," Austin said tightly. "So why don't you just—"

"Fergus!" Izard said.

Fergus stuck out both hands and planted them on Austin's shoulders. He squeezed his fingers and pulled Austin up until his feet left the ground. He dangled there like a rag doll.

"Now what was you sayin'?" Izard said. "Make him

whimper, Fergus, just like Georgiana's doin' over behind the church."

Fergus squeezed his fingers tighter—but there was a loud thump and just as quickly his hands sprang open. Austin hit the ground with Charlotte tugging his sleeve.

"Run!" she cried.

Austin did, right after her, right out the gate. He turned only once—to see Izard close on his heels and Fergus still in the graveyard clutching his shin.

Charlotte disappeared into the woods like a frightened fawn. Austin took longer, but Izard only followed them to the edge of the woods, where he stood shouting "You ain't seen the last of the Wydells!" until they were out of earshot.

When the house was in sight, they stopped and leaned, heaving, against a red maple.

"Did you kick him?" Austin asked.

Charlotte nodded.

"Good. I don't know what would have happened if you hadn't."

Charlotte's golden eyes widened. "They were just . . . young . . . like us."

"They aren't like us, Lottie," Austin said. "I think one of them—"

But he stopped. *How can I tell her I knew Uncle Drayton might be in danger, but I didn't say anything?* he thought. *She'll hate me for sure.*

It doesn't matter. I'm putting Jesus first now. I'm changing. It won't happen again.

"One of them is mean and the other one's strong," Austin said. "I don't think we're a match for them."

"But neither one of them is smart—like you," she said. "You would have talked us out of it if I hadn't kicked him."

Her eyes sparkled. "Of course, it's kind of hard to talk when you're hanging up like the laundry!"

"Did you see that? That boy is a horse!"

Charlotte nodded. "That Izard boy—what a funny name!—he said they were working for that awful Mr. Rhett. At least we won't have to see them. Mr. Pryor said they were traveling around."

"Just passing through," Austin said. And inside, he melted into a puddle of relief.

It seemed that Charlotte was right. They didn't see the Wydells the next day or the following day or for many days after that. And what with getting used to the new routine in the Ravenal summer house, Austin didn't even think about them.

He woke up every morning to the birds, all taking turns making their different sounds—some of them warbling, others twittering, still others squawking impatiently. Then he'd sit up and look out one of the windows and gaze at the mountains. Most mornings the fog rolled from them like an ocean tide coming in. Other times a thin mist hid them like a teasing veil. Once in a while the sun had burned a clear path for him to see hill after hill, as if they would never end. He could never get enough of looking at those mountains.

Charlotte, Austin, and Jefferson could barely take time for breakfast, because morning was their time with Henry-James. Uncle Drayton always had letters to write and business to do then, so Henry-James was to "look after" Jefferson.

Their games took them down to the lake or up the mountain or through the bamboo grove. Austin never suggested that they go to the cemetery. Henry-James would have done it, but he'd have been terrified the entire time.

There were too many other fun things to do, like have a picnic on a shelf of granite they found in the side of a hill or pretend they were stranded on top of Big Glassy Mountain or run errands for Josephine, Mousie, and Ria to the little blue post office or Harper's store on High Road.

Austin loved the day they delivered Aunt Olivia's tea invitations in a rented buggy, with Henry-James driving the horses, to Mrs. King at Glenroy, Mrs. Reed at the church rectory, Mrs. Vincent at Teneriffe, and Mrs. Farmer at the hotel.

"I feel so free today!" Austin said to Henry-James as they trotted through Flat Rock.

"You always free, Massa Austin," Henry-James said.

"But this is different. There's nobody watching over us or telling us to do this or be there."

"There ain't no Patty Rollers, and I likes that," Henry-James admitted.

"It just *feels* different," Austin said. "I just feel freer inside."

"Daddy 'Lias, he say that's where we free anyways. Right inside where the good Lord be."

Sometimes on their travels, they would spot Kady hiding somewhere on the property with her poetry notebook and her fat pencil. They never disturbed her.

They would also spot Polly and Tot strolling across the bridge with their parasols like a pair of grand ladies or lying on their stomachs in the grass, looking at books full of pictures of fine clothes and houses. They always disturbed *them*, perhaps with a shower from a bag full of rhododendron blossoms or simply by sending Bogie to them with a big, slimy chew bone.

Sometimes they even came across Ria and Mother out

walking in the sun. The first time that happened, Austin stopped with his mouth hanging open. Even Bogie wrinkled his already-wrinkly forehead even more and went over to sniff her hand.

"Mother, what are you doing out here?" Austin said.

"Have you seen those big, *shiny* blackbirds, my love?" she said. "They're so black, they're almost blue!"

And then she strolled on with Ria as if she *hadn't* spent the entire winter in bed.

After that, the sight of his sickly mother standing on the side of a mountain, laughing into the breeze, only made him grin.

On the rare days when it rained, it wasn't even so bad being inside. Aunt Olivia was too busy preparing for her tea to even notice they were around. The children would read with Austin's mother, perched on the windowsills in the Hutchinson Room, which they discovered were wide enough to sit on. Or they would go down to the cellar and help Josephine spread molasses, flour, and poison on brown paper to kill flies. Or they would sit on the stairs and plan their next day's game.

Whenever they were in the house, Austin heard singing and humming. He could never figure out where it was coming from, but he liked it. It was the same kind of pleasant background music the birds created for them outside.

They were gathered on the stair landing one afternoon when Ria passed them on the way up with a pile of Sally Hutchinson's clean bed linens. Austin was holding forth about an idea for playing Cherokee Indians when he stopped in mid-sentence and listened.

"Ria!" he said. "Is that *you* singing?"

She stopped and gave him her usual cool look. "Yessir,

Massa Austin. Is that botherin' you?"

"No!" he said. "I just never knew you liked to sing that much."

"Well now, it looks like there is a *few* things you doesn't know, Massa Austin," she said. " 'Scuse me for sayin'." She started to go on up the steps, but she paused and looked back down over her shoulder. "Somethin' 'bout livin' in these close quarters, it make me think we all gon' know more than we did when we come here."

Austin watched her go up the stairs, singing to the sound of the rain on the roof.

In the afternoons, Henry-James had to put on his green house servant suit and wait on Uncle Drayton while Jefferson took a nap. That's when Austin and Charlotte raced through the woods to the cemetery to pick up where they'd left off the day before in the ongoing play about Charlotte Anne and A. T. Hutchinson.

At first, Austin glanced over his shoulder every few minutes to be sure the Wydells weren't around. But they didn't reappear, and soon Izard and Fergus were tucked safely into the back of his mind.

Through it all, Austin stopped often—every other minute, it seemed—to capture in his head another "picture-perfect moment." Life was certainly different here in Flat Rock.

And I'm different, too, Austin thought. *I haven't done anything wrong. I haven't told a lie or hurt anybody's feelings.*

I'm putting You first, Jesus, he prayed every night. *And Daddy Elias was right—everything is going to be all right.*

Things were perfect. He was sure of it.

Until the day of Aunt Olivia's tea party.

It was Sunday and they all donned their best clothes for church first thing in the morning. It was hard to put on his blue velvet suit again after running around all week in light clothes and bare feet, but Austin made it all right by carefully pinning the flag pin underneath his collar.

For Father, he thought as he patted it down.

Although Austin had been to the graveyard almost every day with Charlotte, he hadn't been inside the church yet, and he was gawking as usual as they stepped through the doorway. Just as he was gazing at the three stained-glass windows behind the altar and at the high pulpit on the right that looked as if Moses himself were going to step up into it, Polly hissed to him.

"You have to sit in the back. You and Jefferson and Henry-James—that's where all the boys sit."

He looked where she was pointing at the two benches that stretched across the back of the church and tried to smother a smile.

I'd rather sit back there with Henry-James than up here under Aunt Olivia's eagle eye, he wanted to say to her.

Instead, he just whispered, "What about Charlotte?"

"She'll sit with the ladies, of *course!*" Aunt Olivia said. And then she assumed a graceful smile and took Charlotte gently by the hand.

What a performance, Austin thought as he watched her lead Charlotte, Polly, and Kady up the aisle with her silky lavender gown swishing and her plumed hat held high. *She pretends better than Lottie and I do!*

Polly had a show of her own going on. Right across the aisle from her, there was a boy of about 15 with curly hair the color of coffee, wearing a tan summer suit that accented his sturdy shoulders. Austin saw him glance at Polly and smile politely. That was all Polly needed. From then on, she spent more time dropping her handkerchief and peeking at him from under her hat than she did looking at the preacher or the prayer book. Austin rolled his eyes in disgust.

Henry-James was interested in other things. The minute the three boys sat on the back bench, Henry-James leaned over and whispered, "I likes this church."

"Why?" Austin whispered back.

"Looky there."

He nodded toward the congregation, and Austin studied it for a minute before he felt a smile dawn on his face.

"The slaves are mixed right in with the white people!" he whispered.

Henry-James nodded, his lips curved into a satisfied smile. "That's why I likes it."

But as Austin looked out over the congregation again, he noticed something else. The women sitting in their narrow, gated pews were all whispering and pointing . . . and they seemed to be pointing at Aunt Olivia.

Austin watched them closely. From under their flowered, wide-brimmed bonnets, they cut their eyes toward her, glittering with untold gossip. Lips curled, mouths pressed, and nostrils flared, as if not one of them could bear to wait to say out loud to each other what they were whispering to their husbands and daughters.

Austin looked quickly at Aunt Olivia. She was smiling up at the altar and patting her hair with a gloved hand and adjusting the ribbon on Polly's hat.

She had no idea what was going on behind her back.

I hope those aren't the ladies who are coming to the tea party, Austin thought. *If they are, it's going to be more like a cat fight than a party!*

After the service—which wasn't nearly as lively with its pipe organ music as the ones back in St. Paul's Parish where the slaves set the whole church to rocking with their singing—Austin decided to tell Kady what he'd seen.

I'm not going to make the same mistake I made with Uncle Drayton, he thought.

He dodged around Polly, who was whispering to Aunt Olivia, "Who is that adorable young man with the curly hair?"

"That's Reverend Reed's son, Randall," Aunt Olivia cooed. "Do you have an eye for him, Polly?"

Austin rolled his eyes once more and caught up to Kady just as she was approaching the carriage.

"Kady," he whispered, "did you see how those ladies—?"

But before he could get out the rest of the sentence, there was a clattering on the drive and enough pounding of horses' hooves to send up a cloud of dust.

"Oh, my!" Aunt Olivia said from the hill. "What is *that?*"

"Ladies and gentlemen! Neighbors!" a voice called out.

The rattling wagon came to a halt, and Austin hurried out from behind the Ravenals' carriage to get a glimpse. And when he did, he choked.

There were two men standing in the back of the wagon. One was tall with long, greasy hair, which he jerked away from his face with a toss of his head.

That's where Izard Wydell got that hair-tossing thing, Austin thought. *That's Roger Pryor!*

But it was the other man who scared him more. Tall, long-legged—it was Mr. Eyebrows Rhett.

And behind him crouched his three helpers.

Izard, Fergus, and Georgiana Wydell.

✝ ✝ ✝

Chapter Twelve

Austin could feel Charlotte and Henry-James edging close behind him.

"It's that man," Henry-James whispered.

Austin turned his head. Henry-James's eyes were bulging.

"And those boys," Charlotte whispered.

"What boys you talkin 'bout?" Henry-James said.

"Mr. Virgil Rhett!" a distinguished-looking man with gray hair called out. "I thought you were out preaching your secession sermons to the North Carolinians!"

"This is North Carolina!" Rhett called back.

"But we're all South Carolinians!" said another man with a thick mustache. "We invented secession!"

Light laughter arose from the crowd gathering in front of the church. Mr. Eyebrows Rhett scowled at them all.

"This is no laughing matter, neighbors!" he cried. "There are some among you who still need convincing that the South must secede from the Union or lose all its freedom—and I intend to stay in Flat Rock until every last man is won over!"

As if Mr. Rhett had pointed his finger, all heads turned, and every eye came to rest on the Ravenals. Aunt Olivia gasped and put her hand over her mouth, and Mousie fumbled in the sleeve of her mistress's lavender gown for a hanky.

"What are they looking at?" Jefferson said loudly.

"A very good question, young man!" Rhett shouted, eyebrows tangled. "We are looking at a man who until a few months ago was a pillar of the southern way of life and now has turned traitor!"

"Why don't you just say it, Virgil?" Uncle Drayton said calmly. "You are talking about me."

"You said it, Mr. Ravenal, not me." Rhett looked over the crowd. "Is there anyone else here who does not feel that we have the right to withdraw from a government that has injured us—the very government we helped to create?"

"We helped create a government that works on compromise, not rebellion," Uncle Drayton said, a little louder this time.

"The day of compromise has passed. There is no place for the South in the Union!"

Behind Rhett, Roger Pryor raised his hands and clapped, starting a smattering of applause in the crowd.

"The North has broken its part of the contract by refusing to return our runaway slaves!" Mr. Rhett raved on. "They are bent on hating and persecuting the South. The government has taken away states' rights—and wants to give the Negroes rights—when we all know blacks are incapable of being citizens!"

With each sentence, Rhett's voice grew louder, and Pryor's rousing of the crowd grew more enthusiastic. The man with the thick mustache even shouted, "Yes!"

Austin glanced nervously at Uncle Drayton. He was still standing calmly, while Aunt Olivia hid her face in her handkerchief, but his mouth was stiff as he said, "Yes, I do believe that slavery has become important to our way of life—"

"It is absolutely vital to civilized living! And if we are to remain civilized here in the South, then there must be a revolution—against a foe as oppressive as the British were in 1775!"

Uncle Drayton's voice finally broke from honey smooth to crackling angry. "You're a Fire Eater!" he shouted.

"I am, and I'm proud of it!" Rhett shouted back. "We have been oppressed here in the South long enough. I burn for the principle of freedom, just as our forefathers did! It is our destiny that we should break away from our oppressors and be free to govern ourselves!"

He finished with a flourish of his hand that once again drew applause and cheering from some of the people in the crowd. Others just looked uncertain, but no one jeered or hissed.

Except Uncle Drayton.

"You'll have the whole South destroyed if you keep this up, Rhett!" he cried. "And you, too, Pryor!"

"I want to save the South!" Roger Pryor said through his pointy nose. "We must secede just to be safe—before there are more northerners like John Brown coming down here and trying to turn our own slaves against us! I don't know about the rest of you, but my wife and I fear for our lives every day. We are terrified that our Negroes, whom we've protected and provided for, are going to murder us in our beds!"

Austin looked at Henry-James.

"What you lookin' at, Massa Austin?" he hissed. "I ain't

never thought 'bout murderin' nobody in my life!"

"You have three daughters, don't you, Mr. Ravenal?" Roger Pryor said.

"I do," said Uncle Drayton.

Aunt Olivia pulled Kady and Polly to her as if a band of slaves were that very moment going to snatch them away. Charlotte hid from her behind Austin.

"Then you will understand when I say that our ties with the Union have to be cut for the sake of future generations. Otherwise, we cannot give our children the kind of life that we have led."

Kady yanked herself away from her mother.

"I don't *want* that kind of life," Austin heard her mutter.

"My hat is off to you, Mr. Pryor!" the man with the thick mustache shouted. "How can we help you?"

"You work on Mr. Ravenal here!" Pryor said, impatiently tossing his hair. Mr. Rhett nudged him, and he added quickly, "And you can contribute to our mission by donating generously as these children here pass the hat."

The Wydells jumped off the wagon and scattered amid the crowd, poking their overturned hats into the knots of people.

"Come on, please, Drayton," Aunt Olivia said through her handkerchief. "I don't want to be humiliated any further—and this wind is mussing up my hair. Can't we go?"

Uncle Drayton nodded and pushed her gently toward the carriage by the elbow.

"Ravenal," said a voice behind them.

Uncle Drayton turned, and so did Austin. It was Pryor, curling his lip.

"Didn't I warn you?"

Austin felt a shiver go up his backbone. *You did warn him,* he thought. *But I didn't.*

"*Psst.* You—A. T. Hutchinson."

Austin looked up to see Izard standing a few feet away, felt hat in hand, straggly hair blowing up in spikes.

Austin shook his head.

"No, I don't want your money, stupid," Izard said. "I just want to talk to you."

"Don't go, Austin!" Charlotte whispered in one ear.

"Who dat boy, Massa Austin?" Henry-James whispered in the other.

Austin didn't want to answer either one of them, so he stepped reluctantly toward Izard. He looked around warily, but Fergus was several groups away, thrusting out the hat with his mouth hanging open.

"What?" Austin said. He blinked against the dust that was starting to swirl with the wind.

"I just wanted to check something," Izard said. He narrowed his snappy little black eyes. "When the wind blew your collar up a minute ago, I thought I saw—"

Before Austin could stop him, Izard reached up a grubby hand and flipped over Austin's collar. The flag pin shone up at them.

"Don't touch that!" Austin said. He slapped Izard's hand away, but he knew he was too late. The boy's face came almost to a point as he looked accusingly at Austin.

"Yankee!" he said through his teeth. Izard turned and looked around wildly. "Mr. Rhett!" he cried.

Austin tore off the other way, barging through a circle of women talking behind their hands. He dashed across the churchyard and then stopped, panting, against the church wall and listened.

There was so much arguing and gossiping and shouting going on that he couldn't tell if any of it was about him yet. He squeezed his eyes shut so he could think.

Uncle Drayton is in enough trouble as it is, he thought. *And I didn't save him last time.*

But this is my pin. Father gave it to me. He wanted me to wear it.

He groped around in his mind for a thought to grab on to.

Daddy Elias would have said to think of Jesus first. But what would Jesus want?

He could hear the pounding of bare feet—and Izard's scrappy voice and Fergus's dull one. Fumbling frantically with the clasp on the pin, Austin darted toward the first section of graves he came to, hoisted himself awkwardly over the fence, and ducked behind a tombstone.

Austin heard the voices say, "Where did that fool go?" and "I think I seen him comin' this way." He dug a hole beneath the pine needles with his finger and stuck the pin in. There was barely time to read the name on the grave marker—Eliza Blake—before the voices came around the corner of the church. Austin waited until they passed down to the next level of the graveyard before he crept out through the gate and took off toward the carriage.

He was nearly there when he heard Polly whine, "There he is, *finally.*" And then from behind him, Izard hollered, "We done found him, Mr. Rhett! There's the Yankee now!"

A hand came down and snatched Austin by the back of his velvet jacket. He wriggled and pulled his arms out of the sleeves—and catapulted himself straight forward into the arms of Roger Pryor.

"Is this the boy you were talking about?" Pryor said.

"Yeah!" Izard said. "When the wind blew, I saw it—a Union flag right under his collar!"

"Austin!" Uncle Drayton said. His voice held the first stirring of alarm.

"Look for yourself," Austin said. "There's no pin on my collar!"

Roger Pryor turned him roughly around, and Rhett grabbed the collar and examined it. He let it go in disgust, as if Austin had committed a worse crime by *not* having it.

"I remember this boy," Rhett said to Uncle Drayton. "He's a sly one, like all those Yankees."

"Sly enough to make you look the fool, Virgil," Uncle Drayton said.

"You are *trying* to make trouble, aren't you, Mr. Ravenal?" Rhett said, his eyebrows so tangled that his eyes were nearly crossed.

"No, if I were trying to make trouble, I'd be wearing such a pin myself. All I want is the freedom to be allowed to work out my decision about slavery and secession in my own mind. And the more you rant and rave—the two of you—the less I believe that I would have that freedom if the South were to become its own independent country!"

Virgil Rhett drew himself up as if Uncle Drayton had just slapped him in the face.

"How dare you!" he said, voice trembling indignantly. "You have insulted my honor, Mr. Ravenal!"

"I don't think that's possible," Uncle Drayton said smoothly. "Because I don't believe you have any honor. Good day, gentlemen."

A gasp went through the crowd, followed by much rustling of silk and whispering behind fans. Virgil Rhett leaped indignantly onto the wagon and stood glaring down at Uncle

Drayton. Without moving his mouth, Uncle Drayton made a clicking sound with his tongue. The wagon horse's ears twitched, and he pranced forward a few steps. The wagon rolled one way and Virgil Rhett staggered the other, nearly pitching headlong onto the ground.

Uncle Drayton shook his head and piled his family into the carriage and wagon and left the church.

Aunt Olivia sniffled and buried her face in Polly's shoulder, but Austin sat up proudly on the seat and looked out the window at the South Carolinians until they disappeared from view.

I guess he told you, he thought as he puffed up his chest. *It* does *work when you put Jesus first. Daddy Elias was right. Even Uncle Drayton is changing!*

But the minute he stepped off the carriage, Uncle Drayton put his long fingers around Austin's arm and pulled him off toward the lake. And from the way he was walking, Austin was sure he wasn't about to be thanked.

When they'd reached the water's edge, Uncle Drayton took him by the shoulders and held him there, so close that Austin could smell his leather-and-lavender scent.

"That boy did see a pin on your collar, didn't he, Austin?" he said.

Austin's mouth turned to cotton, but he nodded.

"Why did you wear it when I asked you not to?"

"I wore it under my collar so no one would see it!" Austin said. He shook his head to try to untangle some of the knots. "I don't understand! You just told everyone there that we should try to hold the Union together!"

"But I am trying to tell them that without arousing any more anger than I have to," Uncle Drayton said. "Don't you remember last spring in Charleston—how rough those men can be? Words are one thing, but symbols like your flag, they raise all kinds of emotions. I am trying to avoid that, for everyone's sake. I have been warned, and I am trying to decide how seriously to take those warnings."

Austin swallowed and looked down at the ground. *Tell him!* his mind shouted at him. *Tell him they've already tried something very, very rough!*

"I appreciate your getting rid of the pin, Austin, however you did it. But from now on, would you just let me handle things?" Uncle Drayton gave his shoulders a squeeze. "You know that I think you are a very smart young man. Certainly I have changed my mind about a few things since you've been with us. But this time, Austin, I think I know best. This may be dangerous, and I don't think you understand what that means."

"But I do!" Austin said. "I've heard . . . I saw . . ."

"Austin, enough." Uncle Drayton's voice bordered on sounding sharp. "I have already upset your aunt to the point of hysteria, partly because I had to step in for you. I know you are only trying to help, but I don't need your help. Please, just have a good time with the children and enjoy your summer. Be a *child* for once, all right?"

He patted Austin's shoulders and flashed a charming smile. "Now I must go calm your Aunt Olivia down before a dozen clucking women arrive and drive her completely over the edge!"

He walked off smoothly toward the house, but Austin didn't move.

Be a child? he thought angrily. *Just do what I'm told and don't argue—and don't think?*

He flung himself down to sit on the ground and jammed his elbows onto his knees and his face into his hands.

My father didn't teach me that. Father wants me to be a grown-up. He wants me to be proud of who I am.

His hand groped at his empty collar.

"How am I supposed to put Jesus first when nobody will let me?" he said out loud.

"Now there's a question I've asked myself a thousand times," someone said behind him.

He turned around to see his mother standing there.

Chapter Thirteen

"It's really all right to talk to yourself," Mother said, leaning over to pick some laurel. "But if you start answering yourself, then you need to worry. May I join you?"

Austin nodded, his mind going in four different directions. She set the armful of flowers on the ground and sat on a rock beside him.

"Look at those mountains," she said as she gazed out over the Blue Ridge. "More beautiful than all the diamonds or fine gowns—"

"Or French Victorian furniture."

Mother laughed and squeezed his arm. "So what's troubling you, my love?"

Austin shrugged.

"Think of a question then. Ask me anything you want."

"How do you put Jesus first?" Austin blurted out.

"Oh," Mother said. "Well now, let me see. I try to do that by ... Hmmm ..." She examined the laurel for a moment. "I think I do it by being sure that what I think is valuable is the same thing that Jesus thinks is valuable."

"Example, please," Austin said.

Mother got an impish grin on her face. "What do you think is valuable to Aunt Olivia?"

"Gowns and furniture and tea parties," Austin said without hesitation.

"Do you think that's what is valuable to Jesus?"

Austin cocked his head. "Jesus didn't even have furniture, did He?"

"No, nor gowns either." She nodded toward the flowers. "Yet Solomon in all his glory was never dressed like these, was he?"

"Another example," Austin said.

"How about Polly? What's valuable to her?"

"Crinolines! And shoes—and boys. I don't think Jesus values those."

"Which explains why Polly is so unhappy most of the time. Kady, on the other hand—"

"She values poetry!"

"Well, and nature and good thoughts and honesty. I think Kady and Jesus are pretty well lined up." She nudged him playfully with her elbow. "Now, what about you? What's valuable to you? That's what you have to know before you can figure out if that's what Jesus wants for you." She smiled softly at him and pushed back a wisp of his hair with her gentle fingers. "You think about it, my love. You do that so well." She stood up. "Now I'd better get these flowers up to Aunt Olivia before she loses her mind completely. You would think the Queen was coming to this tea party."

As it turned out, *nobody* came to the tea party. No buggies came up the drive. No ladies swept through the doorway in their tea gowns to eat Josephine's pecan cakes. No womanly laughter filled the house. There was dead silence all afternoon—except for the sniffling coming from Aunt Olivia's bedroom.

The children decided it was best to stay quiet and out of the way. Austin spent most of the afternoon lying on his back in the yard with Charlotte and Bogie, looking up at the clouds and doing what he did best—thinking.

What's valuable to me? That's easy—my pin. What it stands for, that's what Daddy Elias said. Father being proud of me. Not covering up what I believe and being allowed to say it.

He sat up in the grass so abruptly that Bogie lifted his head from a nap and squinted at him.

Isn't that just what Jesus did? Austin thought. *That's it!*

He rolled over on his stomach and poked Charlotte.

"That one there looks like a big sheep," she said, pointing up.

"It does," Austin said without looking. "But Lottie, I want you to help me with something."

"What?" she said. She came up on one elbow.

"I want you to go with me to the graveyard so I can get my pin back."

"You mean, you were wearing it after all?"

"Under my collar, but the wind blew it up. Anyway, I buried it in the cemetery so your daddy wouldn't have to get into an argument, which he did anyway—"

"So why do you want it back?" she asked.

"Because it's what's valuable to me," he said. "Will you help me?"

She sat up with an anxious look twisting her face. "What about those children, the Wydells?"

Austin frowned. "Hmmm. It would be no good if they showed up."

"No good? It would be awful!"

Austin lay back down to study that.

"'Scuse me for sayin'," a voice said from above them. "But if'n you gets grass stains all over that there shirt, you gon' look mighty messy come next Sunday."

Ria passed them, swinging a basket.

"Where are you going?" Austin said.

"It's Sunday and my time off, Massa Austin," Ria said. "I's goin' down to the water to do a little weavin' on a basket and maybe a little weavin' on a story."

"She does tell good stories," Charlotte said when she was gone. "Almost as good as Daddy Elias. That one she told on the train made my blood run cold."

"Wait!" Austin cried.

Charlotte jumped. "Wait for what?"

"That story Ria told about the graveyard. Lottie, I think that might be just the thing to teach the Wydells a lesson— *and* get my pin back." He scooted closer. "I think I feel a plan coming on."

By sunset that evening, the plan was set, and it looked as if everything were going to go their way.

Polly had been more than willing to go on the errand Austin asked her to do that afternoon—delivering a note for the Wydells to Reverend Reed's house, since he would know where they were staying. In fact, her eyes sparkled and she smiled a rare, though brown-toothed, smile when Austin hinted that surely Randall would be there. When she and Tot came back, Tot reported that the mission had been accomplished.

After a whole day of being up and out, Sally Hutchinson

went to bed early, and Ria retired to the cellar with the other slaves. Kady sat on the front porch, composing more poetry. Uncle Drayton tried to comfort Aunt Olivia by taking her to a party at the Farmers Hotel.

"I'm sure this was all a misunderstanding, darlin'," Austin heard him say as they stepped into their buggy with Henry-James at the reins. "You must have put the wrong date on the invitations. You'll see."

As soon as the hoofbeats disappeared down the drive, Austin and Charlotte crept down the stairs to the cellar, armed with Aunt Olivia's black lace shawl, a cane, and Bogie. Austin was nearly bursting at the seams with anticipation.

"I hope they do show up," he whispered to Charlotte as they headed for the back door. "They deserve this!"

"Who's there?" a clear voice said from the other end of the cellar.

"Ria!" Charlotte mouthed to Austin.

He nodded and hurried her and Bogie out the door. They were well into the trees before they heard it open again and then close.

Austin's heart was pounding, but he grinned at Charlotte through the darkness. "That made it more exciting, didn't it?" he said.

"I'm not sure," Charlotte said. "I've never lived in the house with Ria before. I don't know what she would do if she caught us."

"I don't think we'll ever have to find out," Austin said. "We've got this all planned out, remember?"

But the plan hadn't taken into account how dark it was in the woods at night. Trees that reached their branches down like friendly arms in the daytime were more like groping giants in the dark. Austin stumbled over several tree roots, which sent him sprawling, but Bogie was always patient about waiting until he got up before he led them on. As long as Austin could see Bogie's tail, wagging as it did when he had a purpose, it didn't seem quite so scary.

Until an owl gave a startled hoot from high in a ginkgo tree.

And a deer leapt, wild-eyed, across their path.

And a cloud passed ominously over the already-waning moon.

But each time, after he had caught his breath, Austin reminded Charlotte that this was nothing compared to how scared the Wydells were going to be when *they* got through with them.

"You're going to be disappointed if they aren't there, aren't you?" Charlotte whispered.

Austin had to admit he would be. It was just too good a plan to go to waste.

The graveyard was a puzzle of shadows cast in an even darker night. There were grabbing tree branches and misshapen crosses and overgrown fence spikes that looked like spears across the pathways. Bogie made his way through it all with Austin holding on to his tail and Charlotte hanging on to Austin's shirt.

"It's that one," Austin whispered to the dog.

Bogie sniffed his way to the gate. Austin let them in, and they crept like three thieves to the marker in the corner. His fingers traced the letters on the slab. Eliza Blake.

"I wonder what she died of?" he whispered. "Being only 10 and all."

"I hope it wasn't from sneaking around in the graveyard at night," Charlotte whispered back.

Austin grinned at her. "All right, let's get ready."

Charlotte nodded and ducked behind the gravestone with her mother's black lace shawl. Austin got behind the next marker, which was conveniently a tall, bulky monument, and knelt down with Bogie beside him and the cane in one hand. And then they waited.

The night grew chillier as they stayed still. The ground was damp under Austin's pants, and it sent a dank feeling crawling up his backbone. He wriggled to find a more comfortable position and crunched a little pine cone.

"What was that?" Charlotte hissed.

"Just me," Austin said.

"Do you think they're going to come?"

"Sure, they are," Austin said. "But this is getting boring."

"And scary," Charlotte whispered.

"Maybe I'll dig up my pin while we're waiting."

He made a move to come out from behind the monument, and that's when they heard it—the unmistakable sound of something moving up the drive.

Austin dove back behind the grave marker. Bogie put his nose in the air and sniffed busily. A low growl started in his throat.

"Shhh, Bogie," Austin whispered. "Not yet."

Austin heard a tiny squeak come out of Charlotte, and he bit his lip to keep from laughing. This was going to be perfect.

The movement up the drive turned to footsteps on the path. Austin peeked out and saw three ink-colored forms coming slowly toward them.

"Now," Austin whispered.

Two arms came up from behind Eliza Blake's tombstone,

flowing with a black lace shawl. A tiny voice hissed, "Over here!"

"Glory be!" Austin heard Izard say. "What was that?"

"Want me to get 'em?" Fergus said.

"You don't even know what it is yet, stupid! Just wait a minute!"

"Here, please," Charlotte moaned. "Come help me!"

"Somebody's hurt!" a high-pitched voice piped up.

That must be Georgiana, Austin thought. *At least they let her talk.*

"Hush up, Georgie!" Izard spat at her. "I'll take care of this!"

"Want me to go help 'em?" Fergus said.

"What, and walk right into a trap?" Izard said scornfully.

They moved closer. Charlotte waved her black-clad arms over the grave marker and wailed. "Help me! I wasn't ready to die!"

The figures froze. Austin grabbed Bogie around the muzzle and clapped a hand over his own mouth. This really was too good to be true.

"Help me!" Charlotte moaned, still flapping the shawl. "Pull me out before they drag me down again!"

"Drag you down where?" Georgiana peeped.

"I said hush up!" Izard hissed. But his voice was edgy with fright. It was time.

Austin slowly pulled his hand off Bogie's muzzle and began a soft, low moan in his throat. Bogie stiffened, then threw back his head.

And he started howling.

"Oh, no!" Charlotte groaned.

"What's that?" Izard said.

"They're coming for me! Please, grab my hand and pull

me back before they get me again! You're my only chance!"

All right now, Austin thought, ready to burst. *Just come a little closer, Izard—or Fergus. Just a little closer so I can stick this cane right in your pant leg. You'll be frozen with fright!*

It looked as if Izard had read Austin's mind. As Bogie howled on, louder and louder, Izard inched closer to Eliza Blake's grave. Charlotte's lace-covered hands gripped the top of the marker.

"No!" she moaned. "No, they're taking me!"

Once again, Izard froze, just within arm's reach. Austin shot out the cane.

But a little voice pierced the darkness. "Don't let them take her!" it cried. And a tiny form hurled herself forward, just as Austin came down with the cane. It stuck into her dress like a spear and held her fast to the ground.

Just then Bogie let out the loudest howl yet, and Charlotte's hands disappeared from the gravestone.

"I'm gone!" she wailed.

"Run!" Izard cried. "Run for your lives!"

He bolted toward the gate, stumbling over Fergus, who was fumbling with the latch. Behind them, Georgiana screamed a scream that went down through Austin's innards.

"I can't move!" she cried. "I'm stuck!"

She put her hands out to Izard, screaming in terror. Izard gave her one long look, shouted "Come on, ya little sissy!" and ripped Fergus out of the way. He hurtled through the gate with Fergus on his heels.

"Don't leave me!" Georgiana cried. "Please, don't leave me!"

Austin couldn't stand it. He let go of the cane, and

Georgiana pitched forward. She lay completely still, her head inches from the next gravestone.

Austin crawled from behind the monument. "Are you all right?" he said. His heart was crawling up his throat.

She lifted her head and looked back at him. Her eyes—those big hazel eyes he'd seen a few days ago—widened in horror, and her mouth flew open in a terrified O.

"I-*zard!*" she screamed.

Austin heard the footsteps stop hammering down the path.

"Run, Lottie!" Austin hissed. "Over the fence—and *run!*"

Charlotte was over the fence, lace shawl and all, almost before Austin could get out from behind the monument. Bogie stopped howling and started growling. His paws went up on the monument, and he narrowed his eyes at the fast-approaching forms of the Wydell brothers.

"Get 'em, Bogie!" Austin said. And then he scrambled up onto the fence.

"It's that boy!" Izard shouted behind him. "It's that A. T. boy, Fergus. You get him!"

Austin didn't look back as he jumped from the fence. He only heard Bogie growling and Izard shrieking, "I ain't afraid of you, ya mangy mutt! Come on! I can take you!"

Austin just plowed forward—and went nowhere.

At the same moment he realized his shirt was caught on the fence spike, he felt a big burly hand come down on his shoulder.

"I got him, Izard," a dull voice said. "Now what do you want me to do with him?"

✠ ✦ ✠

Chapter Fourteen

ustin felt himself turn to stone.

"I want you to give him a good whuppin', is what I want you to do!" Izard shouted. "Get off me, dog!"

There was a loud yelp.

"Now don't come at me again or I'll chop them ears clean off!"

Austin shook off his stony state and twisted his head around.

"Don't hurt him!" he screamed at Izard. "So help me, you'd better not hurt him!"

"Or what?" Izard said, his partially toothless mouth hanging cockily open. "What are you gonna do, hangin' from the fence post like an old rag?"

He blurted a laugh and, as Bogie growled and lunged at him, reached out and grabbed Bogie's ear. Bogie yelped again and tried to yank away. Whining and growling down in his throat, he looked helplessly at Austin. He minced back and forth as if he didn't know what to do.

"Leave him alone, I said!" Austin cried. And then he

planted his feet against the fence post and pushed forward as hard as he could. He heard his shirt rip and felt Fergus's beefy hand come away from his shoulder. Izard snatched up both of Bogie's ears.

"Don't take another step or I'll rip his ears off!" Izard shouted.

Bogie whined, and Austin's heart beat its way into his mouth.

"You scared my little sister to death again—and nobody gets away with that twice!" Izard said.

"It wasn't her I meant to scare!" Austin said. "It was you!"

And then he stopped. It was only then that he realized he still had the cane in his hand. With a flail of his arm, he lifted the cane above the fence and brought it down with a crack on Izard's wrist. He let go of Bogie's ears with a yelp of his own.

"Come on, Bogie!" Austin cried.

Bogie cleared the fence in one leap, ears flying out behind him. The two of them tore off down the maze of paths in the graveyard with Bogie in the lead. They took just a few turns before the footsteps stopped behind them and only the yelling continued.

"We'll get you, A. T. Hutchinson! You just see if we don't!"

The words were still ringing in his ears when Austin got to the bridge that led to the Ravenals' house and hung, panting, over the railing. Bogie put his paws up, too, and panted with him.

"At least we got away," Austin said to him. "And we had them going for a while there, didn't we?"

Bogie whined and nuzzled at Austin's arm with his nose.

"I know—that scoundrel hurt your ears, didn't he? Let me see those."

But before Austin could take hold of the soft, floppy ears, they perked up, and Bogie looked over his shoulder.

"I hear it, too!" Austin whispered to him. "It's a buggy! It's Uncle Drayton and Aunt Olivia coming home!"

He looked around wildly. They could try to sprint on ahead, but Henry-James was running the horse pretty fast. If he and Bogie went off into the woods—

But there was no more time to think about it. The buggy was rapidly approaching. Austin raced to the other end of the bridge and veered off to the right and down the bank. He'd just landed under the bridge when the horse's hooves began to clatter overhead. Austin slid down beside Bogie. The ground was slick, and suddenly he couldn't stop sliding. He landed with a plop in the lake as the buggy passed over them and went on up the drive.

Austin hauled himself out of the shallow water, shuddering as it soaked through pantaloons, torn blouse, cotton stockings, and leather shoes. He looked down at Bogie, who was shaking himself.

"Well, I won't be sneaking in the front door, that's for sure," Austin told him. "Lead me to the cellar, Bogie."

He was shivering by the time they got to the hidden back door.

"I hope I can find a blanket to wrap in after I take off these wet clothes," Austin whispered to Bogie as he creaked open the door.

"That ain't all you gonna find," another voice whispered to him.

Austin's heart stopped. Ria stepped out of the shadows,

arms folded across her chest and mouth pressed into a firm line.

"Hello, Ria," Austin said, mouth fumbling. "I was just—"

"I know what you was 'just'. I already catch Miz Lottie comin' in. I been waitin' ever since you two young'uns left."

"Oh," Austin said. "Did you tell Aunt Olivia?"

"Not yet," she said. "I ain't tellin' her nothin' till I finds out what you been up to."

"Charlotte didn't tell you?"

Ria cocked an eyebrow as she tossed him a blanket. "She 'bout as tight-lipped when it come to you as she is 'bout Henry-James. Ain't nobody gon' get her to tell nothin' on one of her friends. Now 'scuse me for sayin', but you better get yourself out of them clothes 'fore you catch your death of new-monia."

It didn't occur to Austin not to obey. He shed his clothes down to the skin and wrapped in the blanket while Ria turned away and dried off Bogie and sent him to lie down in a corner. She picked up Austin's shirt and surveyed it with a frown.

"I got caught on a fence post," Austin said. "I kind of tore it."

"And I was worried 'bout grass stains," Ria said dryly. "What kind of fence do this?"

Austin's gaze locked on to her scowling face. *I don't think you lie to this lady*, he thought. *She knows the truth before you even say it.*

"Graveyard fence," he said.

"What in the *world* you doin' out in the graveyard in the middle o' the night, child?"

"Playing a trick on somebody," he said. "Somebody who deserved it!"

"Mmmm-hmmm," she said.

"They did, Ria."

"This got somethin' to do with why you thought that stagecoach crashin' was your fault?"

Austin looked at her sharply. He *had* said that in front of her that day.

"Well, I don't know nothin' 'bout that, Massa Austin," she said. "I just knows you smart enough to get yourself in a whole lot of trouble. 'Scuse me for sayin', but you gots to learn when to let the Lord do the work."

"I'm trying to!" He swallowed. "Are you going to tell Aunt Olivia and Uncle Drayton? I don't care so much about me, but it was my fault Charlotte went with me."

"And I don't care so much 'bout you either, as I do 'bout your mama," Ria said. "She doin' real well right now, and if'n she get upset over Miz 'Livia shoutin' at her, I'd be right upset myself."

"Me, too," Austin said.

"Then at least you knows what's important, Massa Austin," she said. "Now why don't you go on upstairs to bed, and I'll see if'n I can't do something 'bout this here shirt." She shook her head and walked away muttering. "My boy works in the rice fields, and he ain't never come home lookin' this bad—"

Austin was shivery with relief as he took the stairs. *I'm glad Mother is valuable to her, or I'd be in a heap of trouble right now,* he thought.

He stopped dead halfway up the second flight of stairs. *Valuable!*

He hadn't dug up his pin.

His skin prickled as if a *thousand* flag pins were poking him. He slumped down on the steps.

I have to get it! his mind shouted at him. *It's important to me!*

His first thought was to get into dry clothes and go back out there, but he tossed that aside immediately. Ria would be standing guard over him for the next two weeks!

Maybe Bogie—

No, Bogie was smart, but not that smart. He couldn't do it by himself.

I could wait until morning—

He sighed heavily. What if it was gone by morning? What if the Wydell brothers wondered why he'd gone there and they found it?

"Massa Austin?" a voice whispered from below. "Is that you?"

Austin scooted to the banister and looked down.

"Henry-James!" he whispered back. "Come on up."

Henry-James took the steps two at a time and knelt in front of Austin, still in his braided green house servant suit.

"I thought that was you I saw on the bridge," he said. "Did you go divin' in the lake?"

"I didn't dive in. I fell. I was hiding from Uncle Drayton."

Henry-James sniffed. "He wasn't payin' that no mind. He too busy tryin' to get Miz Olivia to stop bein' hysterical."

"Why?"

" 'Cause everybody at that there fancy party turn they noses up like Missus and Marse Drayton smell like Bogie."

"Then it wasn't a mistake that nobody came to her tea party."

Henry-James shook his head. "She be bawlin' all the way home. I never heard such carryin' on." He looked closely at

Austin. "What was you doin' out there this time o' night, Massa Austin—you and Bogie?"

Austin filled him in. He finished with a sigh. "I don't know if I'll ever get my pin back now."

"You know what Daddy 'Lias would say. If'n the good Lord want you to have it, you get it back."

"What's He going to do, come down with His big hand and give it to me?" Austin said. He stared down at his own hands.

"Miz Lottie!" Henry-James said, looking up as he heard a step creak. "What you doin' up?"

"I couldn't sleep till I found out what happened to Boston," Charlotte said as she crept down the stairs to them. "I wouldn't have left you, but I thought you were right behind me. By the time I found out you weren't, I was too scared to go back."

"That's all right," Austin said. And he told her the rest of the story.

"So now the problem is how to get my pin back," he said when he was through.

Henry-James poked his fingernail thoughtfully into the space between his two front teeth. "You know I'd do anythin' in the world for you, Massa Austin—"

"Anything but go in the graveyard," Charlotte said.

Austin cocked his head. "It's not that scary, Henry-James. Bogie knows the way."

Charlotte poked him.

"What?" Austin said. His heart was starting to beat fast. "We already know nothing can hurt you out there—except the Wydells, and you could take them all on all by yourself if you had to, Henry-James. Does anybody know you're even back yet?"

"No!" Charlotte said. "That isn't fair, Austin."

"You're not really *that* scared, are you, Henry-James?" Austin said.

Henry-James's face flinched, and he looked away.

"Stop it," Charlotte said. "He isn't going, and that's all."

Austin wanted to bite off his tongue. *I wasn't ever going to do that again*, he thought gloomily. "It was a dumb idea anyway," he said.

"It gon' be even dumber if ya'll chilrun don't get yourselves to bed," Ria hissed from below.

Henry-James shrugged and made his way downstairs. Charlotte glared at Austin and stomped off to her room. It was a miserable Austin Hutchinson who crawled onto his cot.

I guess what's valuable to me isn't valuable to everybody else, Jesus, he prayed just before he drifted off. *We'll have to find some other way.*

It was still gray outside when Austin opened his eyes. His mother was sitting up in bed, her head turned toward the door.

"I wonder what that was?" she said.

"What?" Austin said, rubbing his eyes with his fists.

"I heard a bump, like something dropped to the floor in one of the other rooms."

"I'll go see," Austin said.

He padded barefoot down the narrow hall and peeked into Polly's room. She was snoring like a bear from under her quilt.

I'll have to tease her about that later, Austin told himself.

He peered next into Kady's room, but she wasn't even

there. *Probably off writing poetry somewhere.*

But when he stuck his face into the crack of Charlotte's doorway, he gasped out loud. Charlotte was sitting on the floor, wrapped in a cape, hair stringing damply in her face. She was clutching her ankle.

"What's the matter?" Austin said as he hurried in and skidded down beside her.

She gave him a dark look. "I'm trying to get my ankle to stop hurting," she said.

"But how did you—?"

"I was climbing back in my window, and I slipped and jammed it against the chimney outside."

"Climbing back in the window?" Austin said. He looked closely at her face and gasped again. "How did you get so dirty? Where have you been?"

"In the graveyard," she said in a hoarse whisper, "looking for your pin! I kept waking up thinking about you looking so sad and Henry-James looking so ashamed because he couldn't go out there. Then I finally couldn't go back to sleep, so I went out to look for it. And no, I didn't find it."

"What happened?"

"I climbed out the window just fine and got all the way to the graveyard. I was about to start digging for your pin behind Eliza's grave, and then there they were again!"

"The Wydells?"

She nodded. "I think they sleep there, Austin!"

Austin felt a pinch in his chest. "Did they hurt you?"

"No, but they sure scared the bejeebers out of me! They put something over my head—I think it was a pillowcase—and then they starting grabbing things."

"What things?"

She looked down at her feet. "Those bows mama always

makes me wear on my shoes, for one. And Rabbit. I took him with me—" she shrugged sheepishly "—you know, for protection."

Austin sank lower in his seat. "That rabbit was valuable to you."

"I loved it, if that's what you mean," she said. To Austin's dismay, her golden-brown eyes filled with tears. "But it isn't that. They ran away laughing, and when they were gone I pulled off the pillowcase and came home. But I was too afraid to stop and get your pin, Austin. I'm sorry."

Austin swallowed and felt like a donkey. "I wish you hadn't done all that, Lottie. You could've been hurt really bad."

"They're just horrible, nasty boys, though," she said. "I hurt my own self trying to get back in."

"No, you don't know what they're capable of!" Austin cried. "I do! They can do really awful things. People could get hurt, maybe even killed!"

"Is everything all right?" Mother said from the doorway.

She crept quietly in, with Ria behind her. Charlotte and Austin exchanged guilty glances.

"Lottie's hurt her foot," Austin said. "Could you look at it, Ria?"

Ria slipped Charlotte's shoe and stocking off to reveal an angry-looking swollen ankle.

"I ain't even gon' ask how this happen," she muttered.

She chased Austin and his mother out of the room—so she could doctor proper, she said. Mother only asked Austin once if she could help somehow before she patted his arm and said, "I'm always here, my love. Remember that."

Ria obviously wasn't going to let Charlotte out of bed, and Uncle Drayton took Henry-James off with him right after breakfast, telling Aunt Olivia he had "some serious talking" to do with some "serious people."

"I'm going to start with Pryor and Rhett," he said. "They're going to be preaching at the Teneriffe Inn today."

Kady was a mere speck in the distance as she headed up toward Big Glassy Mountain. Even Polly, Tot, and Jefferson were nowhere around. Austin was left alone with thoughts that circled in his brain like taunting fingers.

First you almost get Uncle Drayton killed—and the rest of us as well. Then you about get Bogie's ears ripped off. You put Henry-James to shame. Now Charlotte's gotten hurt. And you still haven't gotten the pin back.

Austin wandered down to the lake with heavy feet. Was this what happened when you put Jesus first? And that was what he was doing, wasn't it? What was valuable to Father— the Union staying together and making sure everyone was equal—was what Jesus wanted, he was sure. And Daddy Elias said that was what the pin stood for.

So shouldn't I wear it? Shouldn't I stand up for what's right?

It had seemed so clear yesterday. The pin was valuable to him, and he should have it back. But now it was almost too complicated to think about anymore.

"Just stop it, Jefferson!" a voice suddenly cried behind him. "Just stop it! I can't stand you today! I just can't!"

It was Polly, somewhere in the fir trees along the lakeshore. Usually Austin would have made tracks the other way. But something was different today. It sounded like she was crying—sobbing even.

"Please, Massa Jefferson," he heard Tot plead. "Just leave her 'lone today. Please!"

Austin went over to the trees and pulled a furry branch

aside. Polly was sitting on the ground like Miss Muffet on her tuffet with her skirts billowing up around her. Her face was in her hands, and her shoulders were shaking. Tot stood helplessly behind her, alternating between wringing her hands and shaking them in the air. Jefferson was in front of them, a bucket of water in his hand.

And he was about to hurl its contents right at Polly.

Chapter Fifteen

"No, shrimp!" Austin called. "Don't!"

He caught Jefferson by the back of the britches and managed to spill the water on the ground. Polly looked up, blinked, and burst into a fresh wave of tears.

"What did you do to her?" Austin said to his brother.

Jefferson shook his tousled black head and squirmed away. "I didn't do anything to her—yet," he said. "Uncle Drayton told her to look after me because he was taking Henry-James off with him, but all she wanted to do was cry, so I was trying to cheer her up."

"By throwing a pail of water in her face?"

"I like it when people do that to me," he said. His lower lip came out in a pout.

"That's because you're an absurd little shrimp," Austin said.

Jefferson crossed his arms firmly and continued pouting. Austin looked down at Polly.

"What's the matter?" he asked.

"What do you care?" she said through her fingers.

Austin shrugged. "I don't know. I just thought you looked about as miserable as I feel, and I just wondered—"

"You can't feel as terrible as I do!" Polly cried. She pulled her hands away from her face and clutched at her skirt. Tears streamed down her face, and her eyes were so puffy that they were almost closed. "Everyone likes you, Austin! You couldn't possibly know how I feel!"

Austin snorted. "Your mother hates me! Your father thinks I'm a bothersome little boy—"

"That's not what I mean! You have friends! I don't have anyone, and I never will!"

Austin was beginning to feel uncomfortable. He wriggled his shoulders and kicked at a pine cone. "You've got friends. You've got Tot, and Charlotte told me this year's going to be your first social season in Charleston. You'll get to have all those beaus you've always wanted."

"No!" she shrieked—so shrilly that Austin took a step backward, and Jefferson put his hands over his ears. "You don't understand! There won't be any beaus! Everyone hates Mama and Daddy because they won't secede from the Union!"

"Oh," Austin said. "And that isn't valuable to you."

She stopped in mid-sob and glared at him. "You think you know everything, Austin Hutchinson. But you don't know anything about me. I care about a lot of things, but what does it matter anyway ... because ... because I'm ugly!"

Austin had always thought that was almost true, but to hear her say it so pitifully brought a lump into his throat.

"You are not either ugly," Austin said. He groped for

something else to say. He even prayed a quick, *Jesus, help me out here!*

"What do you mean?" she said. "You always tease me!"

"Because you're fun to tease. You get so mad, it's just . . . fun."

"It isn't fun to hear someone say I'm the homeliest poor creature he ever saw!"

"I never said that!"

"Randall Reed did!"

Austin blinked. "The minister's son? He said that to your face?"

"No, behind my back." Her face crumpled, and her mouth formed an unhappy upside down U. "When I went to deliver that message yesterday, he was sitting out on the front porch just like I had hoped. He was with his father, and they were talking. I went up and spoke to them, and he smiled at me. It was perfect, the way you said it would be!"

Austin's heart began to sink. "And then what happened?"

"We went around the side of the house, like we were leaving, but I couldn't bear to go without finding out what he thought of me, so Tot and I hid in the bushes."

Austin felt the corners of his mouth twitch, but he bit back a smile. He'd have to imagine later a picture of Polly, dress puffing up like a mushroom, crouched in the bushes.

"And that's when he said it," Polly said. " 'She is the homeliest poor creature I have ever seen in my life.' "

"Randall Reed *said* that?"

"No, his father said it." Polly's eyes filled again. "But Randall agreed. He said, 'Yes, Father,' just like he'd thought it up to say himself!"

She flung her face back into her hands and sobbed. Austin wanted to crawl in a hole.

"I'm sorry, Polly," he said. "Really, I am."

She shook her head, still crying. "No, you're not. You're going to go tell Charlotte, and the two of you are going to laugh your heads off behind my back!"

"I won't do that . . . because this is all my fault."

But Polly was weeping too loudly to hear him. He stood there, hands dangling awkwardly at his sides, feeling every bit as miserable as she did, he knew.

"When is she going to stop crying?" Jefferson said.

His face was crunched up into a frown, and his little fists were punched onto his hips. He was the last person Austin would want to be around if he were crying that hard.

"She'll stop when you get away from her," Austin said suddenly. "Come on, you want to play with me today?"

Jefferson's eyes widened, and he looked behind him.

"Yes, I'm talking to you," Austin muttered. "It's the least I can do for Polly." He looked down at his cousin. "I'm taking him with me."

Polly looked up and stared for a moment before she nodded. Then she wiped at her tears with her fingers, but new ones just came down to take their places. Austin shrugged and walked off, holding Jefferson firmly by the hand. At the edge of the trees, he turned back.

"And really, Polly," he said, "you aren't the homeliest creature I ever saw. There're plenty of girls *far* uglier than you."

Somehow that didn't cheer her up much. She burst into another spasm of sobs. Austin yanked Jefferson out of the trees and ran with him—up the hill and away until they couldn't hear her anymore.

"Where are we going?" Jefferson asked.

"Graveyard."

"What for?"

"To have an adventure. We're going to dig for buried treasure."

Jefferson took off like a shot, calling back over his shoulder, "Come on, Austin, let's go!"

On the way, Austin went over it in his mind again. *"I'm going to start with Pryor and Rhett," Uncle Drayton had said. "They're going to be preaching at the Teneriffe Inn today."*

He and Charlotte and Henry-James had gone there delivering Aunt Olivia's invitations. It was clear on the other side of the county. There was no way the Wydells would show up at the cemetery today. He and Jefferson could dig up the pin and be gone—and nobody else would get hurt this time.

When they arrived at the cemetery, Jefferson bombarded Austin with questions.

"Whose grave is that? How old was he when he died? What do you think happened to him? Could I get that disease? Would I die if I got it? Is there anybody seven years old in here?"

Austin finally hushed him up by dragging him into the Blakes' section and pointing to Eliza's grave.

"She was only 10 years old—between your age and mine," Austin said.

"What did she die from?" Jefferson said, his voice suddenly low and reverent.

Austin wanted to answer, "From asking her big brother too many questions," but he decided against it. He'd already done enough damage to little children's minds in all this. He thought guiltily of little Georgiana Wydell and her big, frightened, hazel eyes.

"Well, are we going to dig her up?" Jefferson said.

Austin jumped. "What?"

"You said we were going to dig."

Austin rolled his eyes. "We aren't going to dig *her* up. We're going to dig up a treasure."

"What treasure?"

"You remember that flag pin Father sent me?" Austin said.

Jefferson nodded.

"It's buried here." He pointed to the spot. "And we have to get it before somebody else does. It belongs to the Hutchinsons."

"It belongs to the devil, is who it belongs to!"

Austin whipped his head around. Izard Wydell stood over him, his black eyes snapping. And beside him was big Fergus with his mouth hanging open and his big fists already doubled.

Austin didn't know which was going faster, his heart or his mind. One pounded in his chest while the other hammered out thoughts in his head.

What are they doing here? They're supposed to be on the other side of the county! And how am I going to get myself—and Jefferson—out of this one?

"Run, Jefferson!" he screamed suddenly. "Get home as fast as you can! Go!"

"But what about the treasure?" Jefferson said.

Izard snatched up a handful of Austin's shirt. He felt every bit as strong as Fergus—and twice as angry. "What treasure?" he said.

"There is no treasure!" Austin screamed. "Just run, Jefferson!"

Whether he did or not, Austin didn't know. Before he

could even turn around, something big and hard hit him full in the face. All he saw were stars.

"Lousy Yankee!" Izard shouted. "Hit him again, Fergus!"

He did, in the stomach this time. Austin doubled over and heaved for air.

"That was for the first time you scared my little sister!" Izard said. "Here's for the second time!"

There was a little peep. Austin heard it just before he felt a beefy hand chop him on the back of the neck.

"And we haven't even gotten to paying you back for wearin' that Yankee pin and stirrin' up all the folks! That's *our* job!"

Austin's hair was grabbed and pulled until it strained at the roots. It brought his head straight up so he could see Izard and Fergus. Izard spat at him, getting him in the left eye. Fergus pulled back his fist and let it fly into his right eye. Just before everything went black, he saw only one other thing—little Georgiana quietly crying and shaking her head.

The first thing Austin thought of—before his eyes even came open—was the girl who was stuck to the ground with a cane. That was because he couldn't move. His arms, his legs, even his mouth were all paralyzed.

But when his eyes flew open in a panic, he saw why. His legs were tied together and stretched out in front of him. The rest of him was roped to something behind him, and it didn't take long to figure out that it was a tombstone. There was something smelly pulled tight around his mouth.

Probably a piece of Izard Wydell's shirt, Austin thought. *He's the dirtiest boy I ever knew—inside and out.*

But that thought left him with a hollow feeling. *I'm pretty dirty myself*, he thought. *Now they've got the pin, and there will be no end to the trouble . . . for everybody.*

It was only then that something struck him, hard, right in his thoughts.

That stupid pin isn't what's valuable at all! And I've hurt everybody just because of that pin!

He strained against the ropes, but the Wydell brothers had known what they were doing. Only somebody as strong as they were could get him out of this.

Austin looked around miserably. He figured it was almost noon from the position of the sun. The Wydells were probably long gone with his brother by now. They'd knocked Jefferson out, too, for sure, or he'd have kicked every one of their shins black and blue and driven them crazy with questions.

Austin tried to smile at that, but his insides were aching. *I tried to put You first, Jesus,* he prayed. *But I guess I didn't know how.*

He could feel something trickling out of his nose. He blinked hard to keep anything from trickling out of his eyes. He tried to think about something else—anything—to keep from crying.

Austin craned his neck to look around. He was still in the same section. There was the big monument beside him. That in itself was chilling. He was tied to Eliza Blake's tombstone.

He shivered that thought off and closed his eyes. Think about how to get loose, that's what he should do. If he could only call for help, someone over at the rectory might hear him. He gnawed at the cloth over his mouth. It tasted as bad as it smelled, but he kept biting and pulling at it with his teeth.

All he got was a mouthful of foul-tasting threads. He was

stretching his neck down to his chest, trying to rub the gag off against the ropes, when he heard something. No, it was a some*body*. Then he realized it was *several* somebodies. They were coming up the drive, with hard, angry steps.

Austin felt his whole chest caving in. They were coming back.

The Wydells were coming back.

Chapter Sixteen

ustin's mouth turned to sawdust against the gag. He wrenched his shoulders violently against the ropes and kicked both legs until there was a heel-hole in the ground. But the ropes didn't budge.

And the footsteps were getting closer—and faster.

It was clear that he could pull and strain all day and never get loose. Austin got still and tried to think.

I can't get away.

But I don't want them to beat me up again.

How can I keep them from beating me till I'm dead?

And then the answer was there.

I'll pretend to be dead already.

As the hurried pounding of feet grew louder, Austin slumped over the ropes and closed his eyes.

For a few minutes, the footsteps were scattered and halting. Then they stopped altogether. Austin sucked in his breath and held it.

There was a long silence that hung over Austin's head like a sword. He had to force himself not to look up and see what they were doing. Instead, he prayed, as fast and as hard as he could, *Lord, please help!*

And then the graveyard silence was ripped open so sharply that Austin jerked against the ropes.

"There he is!"

"Austin!"

"They done hurt him—bad!"

Those weren't the voices of the Wydells that surrounded him. It was Kady, Charlotte, and Henry-James. Austin jerked his head up and flung it around, shouting for all he was worth under the gag.

"They done tied his mouth shut!" Henry-James cried. He leaped the fence and dodged around a tall cross to get to him. The gag came off with one pull of his big black hands.

"Austin, are you all right?"

Kady was leaning over him, her hair slipping down from a bun and her face flushed from running. She pushed his hair back with both hands, and Austin saw her dark eyes startle wide open.

"I'm all right, but they took Jefferson! You have to find him!"

"He found *us*," Kady said. "Although it took a while to get out of him where you were. The poor little guy was so terrified, he could hardly speak. For a Hutchinson, *that's* terrified."

Charlotte limped to Austin's other side and stared. "Where's all that blood coming from?" she said. Her own blood was quickly draining from her face.

"He hit me right in the nose—Fergus did," Austin said.

"That isn't the only place," Kady said. "You're getting one beauty of a black eye." She lifted her brown checkered skirt and ripped off a strip of petticoat. "Lottie, honey, hobble on down to Mud Creek—beyond those last graves behind the church. Get this full of water, would you?" She shook her head down at Austin. "I'm not going to have a single petticoat left if this summer keeps on the way it's going now."

"I'm sorry," Austin said. "It's my fault."

"As if I cared two bits for petticoats anyway," she said. "Have you got those ropes untied yet, Henry-James?"

Henry-James gave a final grunt and produced both ends of the rope that had held Austin to the gravestone. He went to work on the leg ropes while Kady examined Austin's arms.

"They don't hurt," Austin said. "It's my stomach—and the back of my neck."

Kady put a gentle hand on Austin's belly, and he winced. She frowned and shook the rest of her hair out of its knotted bun with a toss of her head. Dark strands fell untidily across her shoulders. "Who was it that did this to you? We couldn't quite make out what Jefferson was telling us, though Lottie seemed to know."

"The Wydell brothers," Austin said. "They're the ones working for Mr. Rhett and Mr. Pryor."

"Ah, that explains it," Kady said.

"They've had it in for me ever since the first day I saw them, right here in this graveyard. Then yesterday, when they saw me with that pin, that really set them off."

"But I don't understand why you came back here."

"I didn't think they'd be here. I thought they'd be at the Teneriffe Inn."

Kady shook her head. "No, what did you come here *for?*"

Austin looked painfully down at his knees, now free from the ropes. "For nothing," he said.

Charlotte hopped up on her good foot, huffing for

breath, and handed the wet rag to Kady, who went to work on Austin's nose.

"So, did you find it?" Charlotte said.

Austin could hardly look at her. "I never even got the chance to look," he said.

"Do you want me to?"

Austin shrugged. Charlotte looked at him for a minute, and then she disappeared behind the tombstone. She came back a moment later, shaking her head. To Austin's own surprise, he didn't even feel sad—or angry. He just felt stupid.

"Except for a black eye and a bloody nose and a tender belly, I think you're still in one piece, Austin," Kady said. "Let's get home, huh? If Jefferson ever actually did fall asleep, he'll be up from his nap soon, and I don't think Polly is going to be much good to him. She hasn't stopped crying since yesterday afternoon."

"That's my fault, too," Austin said. "Hey, what are you doing?"

Henry-James got hold of one arm and one leg and hoisted Austin up across his shoulders.

"I's fixin' to carry you home, Massa Austin," he said. "And the sooner I gets out of this here graveyard, the better."

Austin felt a sting go all the way through him. "That's *another* thing that's my fault. I'm sorry you had to come here, Henry-James. I know you're scared of cemeteries, and I don't blame you now. I've had nothing but bad luck in this one!"

"I weren't scared at first," Henry-James said as he took the path like a bolt of lightning. "All's I be thinkin' 'bout was gettin' to you. You come before them fears this time, Massa Austin."

They were almost to the house before Austin thought to ask, "Why aren't you working for Uncle Drayton, Henry-James? Aren't you going to get in trouble?"

"All he want me to do today was bring him the mail from the post office, and then he say leave him alone to do some thinkin'. So I done that, and jus' as I was comin' back, Miz Kady and Miz Lottie be runnin' me down and sayin' they's goin' to the graveyard for to look for you."

"I don't want Aunt Olivia to see me looking like this," Austin said. "She'll have the Hutchinsons on the next train."

So they slipped quietly in the back cellar door and up the stairs to the first floor. But they needn't have worried. The household was far too occupied with something else to notice if Austin had had two black eyes and no nose at all.

From the library at the far front corner of the house, they heard a wailing that outhowled Bogie. Uncle Drayton's voice could barely be heard above it.

"My dear, I am certain the letter is a bluff—designed to scare us off or me into accepting their politics."

"It isn't a bluff!" Aunt Olivia said through her sobs.

Henry-James set Austin carefully on the floor, and the children looked at each other. Kady nodded toward the hall-way, and they all tiptoed in together to listen. They were jammed together so tightly that Austin's chin was digging into Kady's back.

Aunt Olivia was talking in choked sobs now. "You read it yourself, Drayton! They said we were lucky to survive last time. We won't be that lucky again."

"You see, it is a hoax," said Uncle Drayton, trying for the honey-smooth voice. "There was no 'last time.'"

Austin stiffened. Kady turned her head to look at him.

"They've turned their backs on us in church and at

parties," Aunt Olivia said. "They refuse to come to our home. I'm sure they think the only way to break down our stubbornness is to hurt us!"

"This is not about stubbornness. This is about my doing what I think is right."

There was another round of choking sobs. "Is it right to put your family in danger?"

"I'm not completely sure we are in any danger. Men like Pryor and Rhett may have mean tongues, but to attempt . . . murder . . . I don't think so. They come from upstanding families—"

"There are good Rhetts and there are bad Rhetts, and a bad Rhett is like the devil himself! Drayton, I'm frightened for myself and you and our children!"

"You're being ridiculous, Olivia!"

No, she isn't, Uncle Drayton! Austin wanted to cry out. *She should be afraid—and so should you!*

Kady turned around and shoved them all backward. "Go!" she whispered. "Upstairs!"

Behind her, there was rustling toward the library door. The children made for the stairs and were on the second landing when the door came open. They escaped to the second floor just as they heard Uncle Drayton say, "Not a word of this threat-letter to the children. I want to think this through and decide what to do."

Me, too, Austin thought miserably as they made their way into the Hutchinson Room. *I want to think. I have to decide what to do! I can't make any more mistakes!*

"Austin!"

He looked up at his mother, who had come out of her chair by the window and was already going white-faced. Beside her, Ria frowned and marched toward him.

"Have you been *fighting?*" Mother asked.

Ria took his face in her hands and peered closely at his eye.

"No, *I* wasn't fighting," Austin said. "*They* were."

"Is he all right, Ria?" Mother came over and joined in the scrutiny. The concern on both of their faces made Austin feel worse than ever. He shook away from them and slumped over to his cot. Jefferson was curled up on it like a kitten, sound asleep.

Behind him, Kady and Charlotte told Austin's mother the story. When they were finished, she sat on the edge of the bed and ran a cool hand across his forehead.

"All that for a pin you lost in the end anyway," she said.

"I know," Austin said. "I'm stupid."

"Oh, far from it," Mother said, eyebrows shooting up. "I think you're smart enough to know what you've learned from all this. Why don't you tell me?"

Lying down, Austin put his hands behind his head and stared at the ceiling. "I figured it out while I was tied up. What's valuable to me wasn't the pin at all—it was all of you. And I hurt almost everybody because I thought that was what you meant when you said what's valuable to you tells you what to put first."

"But see, you've already learned that, Austin," Kady said. She turned from the window and pushed her hair out of her face. "The first thing you said when I took that gag off of you was 'Jefferson!' And then you were all concerned about Henry-James being afraid in the graveyard and getting in trouble with Daddy."

"Now you know, my love," Mother said. She smiled down at him. "Now you won't make the same mistake again."

That should have made him feel better, he knew. But a

lump the size of one of Josephine's dumplings was growing in his throat. He turned over on his side to hide his face.

Mother sighed and passed a hand through his hair.

"Want me to read to you, Aunt Sally?" Kady said.

"Yes, do," Sally Hutchinson said. "Read me some more of your poetry."

He could hear Kady thumbing through her notebook and Charlotte climbing up onto Mother's bed beside her and Henry-James shuffling over to the doorway in his heavy man-servant boots and leaning against the door frame.

In her full, rich voice, Kady began to read.

She finds the music in everyday things
In rusty gates and raindrop pings
In rocking chair squeaks and wagon wheel spokes
And piglet squeals and bullfrog croaks.

As Kady read on, Ria began to hum softly from her place in her chair, keeping a rhythm with the patting of her foot on the wood floor.

You may find joy in opera songs
Or symphony strains or choir throngs
But I'd rather listen, my head in my hand,
To her deep throaty hum with her everyday band.

"That was about Ria, wasn't it?" Charlotte said.

"It was," Kady said.

The room fell quiet. A breeze kicked the lace curtains out over the cot, tickling Jefferson's face and making him sigh softly in his little-boy sleep. Austin couldn't even swallow because of the lump in his throat.

This is another picture-perfect moment. Except for one thing.

And he wanted so much for it to be right.

He sat up on the cot, joggling Jefferson's eyes open.

"What is it?" Mother said.

"I've messed something up really badly," he said. "I have to go talk to Uncle Drayton—right now."

He found him still in the library, standing at the window, staring out over the lake below. He didn't turn around when Austin said, "Excuse me, sir."

"I don't really have time to chat right now, Austin," he said. "I have some things to think through."

"I know." Austin took a breath. "I was listening. And that's why I'm here. I know something—"

"You know very little, actually, Austin," Uncle Drayton said. He turned around then, and there were two angry red spots, one on each cheek. His eyes looked tired and snappish, and they didn't even register Austin's black eye. "And unless you can tell me without a doubt whether to believe what I read in that letter, you know absolutely nothing that interests me at this moment!"

Austin was stung—but he took another breath. *What's valuable to me—remember what's valuable to me and Jesus.*

"I *can* tell you, sir," Austin said. "The 'last time' they talked about in the letter—that was the stagecoach wreck. I know you thought it was an accident, but it wasn't. I heard the men saying something about it on the train. And then I heard Mr. Pryor giving Fergus some kind of instructions at Greenville—and then I saw . . . I saw Fergus under our coach the night before we left Greenville—only I didn't tell you because Bogie chased him out and I thought it would be all right—and I was mad at you for what you did to Henry-James at the inn. And I didn't know Fergus had a smart little brother who gave Bogie a bone and shut him in a stall—and I suppose they went back and cut the straps on the coach like the driver said someone did. I didn't tell you about it because I thought since we were all safe it didn't matter, and I didn't want you to think I was bad, but it turns out I was because I didn't put what was really valuable to me first and now I've made it worse because I buried the pin in the graveyard and then everybody got hurt or almost hurt trying to get it back for me."

Uncle Drayton crossed the room in two strides and took him roughly by the shoulders. "Just tell me this—did you see Pryor's boy under the coach the night before we left Greenville?"

"Yes, and I heard Mr. Rhett talking to him. He said something like, 'Mr. Chesnut gave you your instructions? See that you follow them to the letter. And report back to me when you're through.' " Austin ducked his head. "I'm sorry I didn't tell you before."

Uncle Drayton ripped his hands away and whirled toward his desk. He leaned there, puffing like a locomotive.

And then he picked up a silver candlestick holder and hurled it across the library. It crashed into the bookcase and slammed to the floor.

Uncle Drayton stood looking at it while the color faded from his face.

"Leave me alone now, Austin," he said. "Just leave me alone."

⚜ ⚜ ⚜

Chapter Seventeen

They were all still there in the Hutchinson Room when Austin returned, and Jefferson was wide awake. When Austin came in and sat, frozen, on his cot, Jefferson moved to his mother and hid his face in her lap.

Austin let all the air out of his chest, and his hands were still shaking. "I'm sorry I even took you to the graveyard, Jefferson," he said. "Don't you be mad at me, too, all right?"

Jefferson shook his head in his mother's skirts.

"I don't think he's mad at just you," Kady said. "He's been grumpy ever since he opened his eyes."

"Here, Massa Jefferson," Henry-James said. "You want this?"

He reached inside his green jacket and pulled out a small, brown object.

"That's the dog Daddy bought you," Charlotte said.

Henry-James held out the tiny animal. Jefferson looked up sullenly, held out a chubby hand, took the dog, and stuck his face into his mother's lap again.

167

"What I don't understand," Kady said, as if she were picking up a conversation where she'd left it off when Austin came in, "is how people like Mr. Rhett and Mr. Pryor—and even those boys—get to be so mean. Why does that happen?"

Austin listened halfheartedly. All he could really think about was the candlestick flying angrily across the room—and the disappointed ache in his own chest.

"I don't think we ever know that for sure," Sally Hutchinson said. "There can be so many reasons. But in this case, I think it might be because there's something they need or think they need that they aren't getting. They get angry and they reach out and just take it. That could be part of it at least."

"I believe that," Ria said. "Ain't never been a slave took nothin' from his massa 'less he mad or hungry."

They suddenly had Austin's attention.

"Uncle Drayton said that—that day we were packing and the peddler came along," Austin said. "He said he bought all the slave children gifts because if they didn't want for anything, they wouldn't steal from him."

"You think that's why those boys took my shoe ribbons and Rabbit?" Charlotte said.

"I think that's part of the story I missed," Mother said, cocking an eyebrow at Charlotte. "But I think those children are so poor and so deprived that they're angry enough to take anything."

"You mean, they wouldn't be like that if they had as much as we do?" Austin said.

"Maybe. Like I said, there are a lot of reasons. But it's possible."

Austin's mind began to spin. *Why should I care why the*

Wydells do all the hateful things they do? he thought. *They practically beat the stuffings out of me. They can go naked for all I give a hoot!*

But Daddy Elias wouldn't want me thinking that way, he thought as his mind spun even faster. *And neither would Jesus.*

But I'm not like Him! Austin thought stubbornly. *I can't do all that good stuff like He did!* Yet he could almost hear Daddy Elias saying, "Mmmm-mmmm, Massa Austin."

By now he was feeling dizzy. If he didn't stop his mind from spinning and decide what to do, he was going to fall on his face. And it was pretty clear what he needed to do, even if he didn't like it. Black eye or not, he had to at least try to put Jesus first.

"I think I have an idea," he said out loud.

"Uh-oh," Kady said, grinning.

"Austin," said Mother, "last time you had an idea, you nearly got your eye socked out."

"No, this idea won't hurt anybody. I'm done with all that."

Ria grunted.

But Sally Hutchinson folded her hands and nodded. "Well, we can at least hear it."

By the time Austin finished telling it, heads were nodding, even Ria's.

"May we do it?" he said. His eyes begged his mother. So did Charlotte's and Henry-James's and Kady's. Only Jefferson went over to a corner and sulked.

"We'd even let Jefferson help," Austin said.

But Jefferson shook his head and looked into the corner.

"All right," Mother said. "As long as you take Kady with

you . . . and Charlotte is careful about her ankle . . . and nobody veers from the plan."

"There will be no veering!" Austin said, scrambling up to his feet so fast it made his head pound.

"What's veering?" Charlotte said.

"What you all usually do," Kady said. "Come on, we have work to do."

While Mother went downstairs to take care of her part of the plan, Kady, Austin, and Charlotte began to dig through their belongings. The guideline was to collect anything they hadn't used that summer. The pile in the upstairs hallway was half as tall as Charlotte when they were through.

"I'm sorry I ain't got nothin' to give," Henry-James said.

"Your part comes later," Austin said. "Don't worry."

Mother reached the top of the stairs just then. "Mr. Rhett and Mr. Pryor will be speaking at Farmers Hotel tonight," she whispered. "And Drayton isn't going. He says he's staying in tonight, which leaves Henry-James free." She smiled and wiggled her feathery eyebrows. "It looks like your path is clear."

It seemed as if darkness would never come that night. Long before the sun set over Big Glassy Mountain, they were dressed all in black with their treasures stuffed into empty flour sacks Ria had scrounged from the kitchen building. Kady checked and doubled-checked and triple-checked the tags she'd penned for each sack: Fergus, Izard, Georgiana.

"Who on earth would name their child Izard?" she said.

But before anyone could venture a guess, Ria appeared in the doorway. "Mousie say Miz 'Livia and Marse Drayton done retire for the evenin'," she said.

The children snatched up their bags excitedly.

"Now, Miz Sally," Ria said, "you sure you gon' answer for Henry-James if'n Marse Drayton come lookin' for him?"

"Absolutely," Mother said. "I know what's valuable, Ria."

So all was ready as Kady, Henry-James, Austin, and Charlotte crept down into the cellar and out the back door and headed down the drive toward the road. Everyone except Charlotte had a pack on his or her back. Charlotte, with her halting walk, carried a pine knot torch to light the way. Once they were out of sight and earshot of the house, Kady said, "Lead us in a song, Henry-James."

And so he did, calling out the words for them to answer as they marched down the road toward Farmers Hotel.

We raise the wheat,
They give us the corn.
We bake the bread,
They give us the crust.
We peel the meat,
They give us the skin.
And that's the way,
They takes us in.

But as soon as Farmers Hotel was in sight, they shushed each other and ducked with their packs behind the long stone wall that bordered the drive.

"Do you see the wagon?" Austin whispered.

Henry-James nodded and pointed. "Right over there, jus' beyond that tree," he whispered back.

"All right, little angels of the night," Kady whispered. "Let's go."

Keeping their backs below the wall, the quartet crept up the drive to the Rhett-Pryor wagon. As planned, Charlotte stood on one foot in a spot where she could see the hotel doorway and keep watch while Kady, Henry-James, and Austin put their big bags into the back of the wagon, with the tags showing.

"They won't know what to think when they look in there and find enough clothes and toys to keep them busy for three years!" Kady whispered. "I wish we could see their faces."

"We could hide here and watch," Austin said.

"Aus-*tin*," Kady said in a warning voice. "You're veering."

Austin grinned and started to follow her and Henry-James down the drive toward Charlotte. But his eye was caught by a light in the window. What he saw there stopped him cold. Quickly, he dove behind a hedge and peeked over the top.

"Austin!" Kady hissed.

"Just a minute!" he hissed back.

The light came from a tin lamp in the middle of a table near the window. The window itself had been thrown open to let the evening mountain air in, and it was easy to see and hear the men sitting there.

Roger Pryor.

Virgil Rhett.

The tall, distinguished man.

The man with the mustache.

Everyone from Charleston—except Uncle Drayton.

Even with Kady hissing insistently in the background, Austin strained to listen. Snatches of the conversation drifted out to him.

"—don't think we'll have any more trouble from the nephew. My boys took care of that—"

"—waste of time. It's Ravenal who votes, not his nephew—"

"—sent the letter—he hasn't replied—"

"And he won't! I say we do it tomorrow—"

"—tonight! The longer we wait, the more stubborn he gets—"

"—and you're sure it will work this time? That stage-coach didn't—"

"—you just leave it to me."

Austin felt a firm hand around his arm. It yanked him out from behind the hedge and down the drive.

"You promised," Kady whispered in his ear. "Now come on!"

"Where are Charlotte and Henry-James?"

"I sent them on ahead. You're determined to stay in trouble 24 hours a day, aren't you? I never saw anybody—"

Her voice stopped short, and she halted him at the edge of the road and stared at him. "Austin, what's wrong?" she said. "You look like you're absolutely terrified. What is it?"

"It's true, Kady!" Austin cried. "It's true. They really are going to do something horrible to Uncle Drayton. I just heard them talking about it!"

Kady searched his face for a moment, and then she nodded. "Come on. You have to tell him, Austin. This isn't a game anymore."

Uncle Drayton stood with his arms folded across the front of his dressing gown while Austin talked from the chair in the parlor that Uncle Drayton had ordered him to sit in. Kady, he knew, was standing outside the door, listening. She was going to run for Austin's mother if Uncle Drayton started throwing heavy objects.

When Austin finished, his uncle shook his head. "These

are men I once called friends," he said, more to himself than to Austin. "You children are more loyal to each other than they are to me."

"That's because they think other things are more valuable than your friendship," Austin said. "And they can't have what they value, so they're angry and they're doing horrible things."

Uncle Drayton looked at him, his eyes sharp. Austin glanced uneasily at the porcelain horse on the table near his uncle's hand.

"You have all the answers, don't you, Austin?" he said.

Austin's mouth went dry. "No, sir," he said. "But I've finally learned who does."

"Who?"

"Well, Jesus, sir."

Uncle Drayton threw up his hands, rocking the horse precariously on its perch. "Just like that. Ask Jesus for the answers. If you think it's so easy, you tell me how to do it, Austin Hutchinson. You tell me one way you've done it."

Austin felt like he had been poked from toenails to earlobes. *I tried so hard to do what was right, to put Jesus first, and I still get yelled at and made fun of. I hate this.*

But he stopped there. He took a breath and opened his dry mouth.

"Just tonight," he said. "We took all the things we don't need and gave them to those poor white children, the ones who have been chasing us and stealing from us and beating us up—well, beating *me* up. Maybe it will stop them from being so angry about what they don't have and then they won't be so mean. Maybe it won't, but at least we put Jesus first, and I thought it might make up for what I didn't do before—you know, telling you about the stagecoach."

Uncle Drayton put up his hand. Austin stopped. His heart was sinking.

"I've heard enough," Uncle Drayton said. "No more. I can't hear any more."

"Daddy?"

Kady was in the doorway, her lips white. "There's a whole train of wagons and buggies coming up the drive. They're waving firebrands!"

Uncle Drayton hurried to the window and pulled the curtain aside. Without a word, he flew to the doorway, nearly knocking Kady down on his way out. Austin and Kady followed him out to the front porch. Below, at the bottom of the steps, wheels were creaking to a halt and men were standing up in the backs of wagons and climbing out of carriages to swing themselves up onto the front steps. Firebrands lit up the night as if it were noontime, each one flickering across a hard face.

This is a picture of hate, Austin thought. He shuddered and clung to the porch railing.

"Well, gentlemen," Uncle Drayton said, his voice coming out in measured spoonfuls. "It seems you have finally decided to call on us."

"This isn't a social call, Ravenal!" Roger Pryor shouted in his reedy voice. He gave his hair a frenzied toss. "This is business!"

"What business would that be?"

"Don't waste your time, Roger!" Virgil Rhett cried. His eyebrows caught in a snarl as he twisted his face at Uncle Drayton. His eyes glittered in the light of his torch. "We'll get right to the point, Ravenal. This is your last chance. You join the secessionist movement tonight, or you'll be sorry you were ever born!"

And with that he hurled his firebrand onto the porch.

⚜

ady screamed and grabbed Austin by the shoulders, pulling him back against the house. Uncle Drayton tore off his dressing gown and threw it over the flames, stomping at them with his shoes until there were only smoldering ashes and smoke on the porch.

The men stood motionless in their wagons. Only their eyes showed life—some astonished, some frightened, some bewildered. Virgil Rhett's eyes alone had a glint of satisfaction.

"There will be more where that came from, Ravenal!" he spat out across the smoky porch.

Austin cringed, and he felt Kady go stiff behind him. There was an urn on the porch. He thought, wildly, that Uncle Drayton might pitch that at Rhett and the others.

But Drayton Ravenal turned to Austin and held out his arm, now bare in the chilly mountain night.

"Come here, Austin," he said.

No! Austin's mind screamed.

But somehow he moved forward. He took his place

beside Uncle Drayton and stared, with eyes that didn't see, over the crowd of men. *Now it's* my *turn to be made a fool of, just like Henry-James was*, he thought.

"Do you see this boy?" Uncle Drayton called out.

"It's your Yankee nephew!" Roger Pryor replied.

"That he is—and he is the reason that I refuse to become a secessionist."

Austin snapped his head up to look at his uncle. Drayton squeezed his shoulder.

"Tonight, he told me something I once knew but had long forgotten—something we've all forgotten because everything is moving too fast and our emotions are becoming too strong. But we'd better remember it or we're going to destroy each other before we ever go to war with the North."

"Get to the point, Ravenal!" Virgil Rhett growled.

There was a murmuring among the crowd. Austin stared from them to his uncle and back again.

"All right," Uncle Drayton said. "Here it is, plain and simple. I see what you're trying to do. You know what you value—the independence of the South—and you're fighting for it. I can appreciate that. But you're doing sinful things to support what you believe, and I will not do that. I will not strike back at you. I'll only do what I think is right. And what is right for me is to try to hold this nation together for as long as we can."

Roger Pryor waved his firebrand over his head. "You expect us to believe that this boy told you all that?"

Uncle Drayton squeezed Austin's shoulder again until Austin thought his arm would drop off. "Not all of that, but enough."

"So you're not with us!" Virgil Rhett cried. "Is that right?"

There was a heavy pause. Uncle Drayton ended it by nodding his handsome head. "That's right."

"Then you're a dead man!" Rhett fairly screamed.

He turned to his companions. But Roger Pryor held up his hand. His eyes were steely as they met Uncle Drayton's.

"It's no use threatening you, Ravenal," he said, his voice hard. "I thought you were made of softer stuff. I misjudged you. But you'll hurt yourself by doing this. You'll see that."

Virgil Rhett looked wildly from Pryor to Ravenal. "What are you saying?"

"I'm saying let's go home, gentlemen," Pryor said. "We'll leave Mr. Ravenal alone. *All* alone."

Virgil Rhett tore off his hat and hurled it to the bed of his wagon like an angry child. The rest of the men silently took their driver's seats or re-entered their carriages and crunched and squeaked their way down the drive. Uncle Drayton stayed on the porch, his hand still on Austin's shoulder, until they were all gone.

Mother, Ria, Henry-James, and Charlotte were waiting in the Hutchinson Room, faces pressed against the window panes, when Austin and Kady burst in. They flew to the two like moths to a candle flame.

"We heard!"

"You saved the day, Austin!"

"Did you get burned?"

"Did Drayton get burned?"

"What happened back at the hotel? What took you so long?"

" 'Scuse me for sayin'," a stern voice cut in, "but if'n we all talks at one time, ain't none of us gon' get no answers."

"Ria's right," Sally Hutchinson said. "Come on, then, up on the bed, all of you—and then we can talk, one at a time."

They piled onto Mother's big bed, with Henry-James sitting uncomfortably on one edge, ready to spring off at any moment. Slowly, as if they were peeling an onion, they sorted out the questions from the answers.

When they were finished, Mother looked for a long time at Austin. She wasn't smiling, but her face had a glow to it.

"Your father would be so proud of you, my love," she said. "You make me feel as if he were right here with me."

Austin shrugged and punched lightly at a pillow. He could have kissed the ground when the door opened and everyone's attention turned that way.

To his surprise, it was Polly in nightgown and lace nightcap, holding a puffy-faced Jefferson by the hand.

"Polly, thank you for taking him into your room so he could sleep a while," Mother said. "Come here, son."

But Jefferson shook his head and looked up at Polly, questions in his eyes.

"Go ahead," Polly said. "I'm telling you it will be all right."

"What will be all right?" Mother said.

Jefferson took in a big breath and marched to the bed. He stood looking at Austin and held out his balled-up hand.

"What?" Austin said.

Jefferson uncurled his fingers. There in his palm was the gold flag pin.

"Where on earth did you find that?" Austin said. He couldn't seem to stop blinking.

Jefferson looked back at Polly again. She nodded.

"I dug it up when you weren't looking," Jefferson said. "When those mean boys first got there." His words got thick. "But then they started to hit you, and I ran. And I was going to keep it for myself, because I wanted it. And I thought it would be all right because I did good sending Kady and Lottie and Henry-James back to get you."

Austin felt something soft happening in his chest. "I think I know what you mean, shrimp," he said. "And it wasn't all right, huh?"

Jefferson shook his head. His bottom lip was quivering. Austin looked at the pin sparkling in the sweaty little palm and at the tears sparkling in Jefferson's eyes.

"Well, it *is* all right now," Austin said. "Why don't you just keep the pin? I could never hold on to it anyway."

Jefferson's blue eyes sprang open. "You mean it? You're not going to yell at me and call me a brat?"

Austin shook his head. "Not over this at least. Something else might come up, of course."

Jefferson could only gaze in awe at the pin.

Polly tapped him on the shoulder. "See?" she said. "I told you he'd understand." She pulled the blue ribbon on her nightcap snugly under her chin and turned toward the door. "I'm going back to bed, if this house is calmed down now. What was all that racket out there, anyway?"

Austin looked around at the pile of people on his mother's bed, all rosy-faced, happy, and warm. All smiling—no one snapping or pouting or angry. Then he looked at Polly, skinny and solitary, standing at the Hutchinson Room door.

"We were just talking about that racket," Austin said. "Do you want to stay and hear?"

She looked back over her angular shoulder. "Me?"

"Sure," Austin said. "There's room."

There was a second's hesitation before Kady said, "Why not?"

Henry-James seemed happy to have an excuse to get up, and as he retreated to a window, Polly took his place stiffly—but with her cheeks taking on color and her lip uncurling.

"Start back from the beginning, Boston," Charlotte said. "And tell it all again."

"Don't leave anything out," Kady said. And then she grinned. "As if you would!"

Austin grinned back. But before he started to tell the story, he took a minute to make a picture in his mind—a photo of a picture-perfect moment.

He'd barely gotten to the part in the story where they dumped the bags in the back of the wagon when Henry-James startled up at the window.

"What's wrong, Henry-James?" Kady asked.

She started for the window, but Henry-James held up his hand. "Better stay back, Miz Kady."

"What on earth?" Mother said. She flung her arms around Charlotte and Jefferson, and at once had Polly in her lap.

"What you talkin' 'bout, boy?" Ria said to her son.

Austin didn't wait for an answer. He bounded for the window and peered out. It took a minute for him to see what Henry-James had noticed in the darkness that stretched down the hillside from the house to the lake. There were two shadows moving across the grass and the sleeping wildflowers. One was short and slight, the other tall. As his eyes grew accustomed to the dark, Austin could see that both were in a hurry, like whatever they were doing was important.

"Who is that?" Austin said.

"Is there someone out there?" Mother asked.

"Look like two boys to me," Henry-James said.

Austin could feel his friend stiffening beside him.

"It is!" Austin cried. "It's the Wydells."

"You sure, Massa Austin?" Henry-James said. "It plenty dark out there."

But Austin didn't need sunlight to know that only Izard Wydell jerked his head that way and only his brother, Fergus, lumbered like an ox.

"That's them," he said. "And I bet they're up to no good."

"Henry-James, get Drayton," Sally Hutchinson said. "Please."

But before Henry-James could move, the darkness suddenly came alive with a harsh light that nearly blinded Austin as it spread across the grass. With slow, awful realization, he saw that it was flames—flames that were spelling something out before their very eyes.

"They're letters!" Kady said, standing behind him. "They're sending us a message!"

Austin felt everyone in the room crowding in around him at the window, but he couldn't take his eyes off the scene below. Slowly, in cruel, fiery letters, the message became clear.

"TRAITOR," he read out loud.

They all held their breath together and watched in horror as the flames licked up at them and reflected themselves garishly against the window glass. It was Ria who finally spoke.

"Somebody better get that fire out 'fore it burn the whole place down," she said.

Henry-James bolted from the room with Austin on his heels. Uncle Drayton was already on the front porch with Josephine and Mousie, who were sloshing wooden buckets down the front steps. Henry-James hoisted up two and charged after them.

"You run to the well and be ready to fill up more as they bring them back!" Uncle Drayton shouted to Austin. "Olivia! Ria! Kady! We need your help!"

Austin tore down the steps and around the side of the house and took off toward the well. As if from out of nowhere, a horse suddenly thundered in front of him, hauling a wagon behind it. He stomped to a halt directly in Austin's path and snorted nervously. In the front of the wagon, a scrappy figure stood up on the seat. Izard Wydell leered down at him, black eyes snapping in the fire-lit night.

"Mr. Rhett told you it weren't over!" Izard shouted. "I bet you didn't believe him, did you, A. T. Hutchinson?"

At first, Austin didn't answer. He was staring at the hat that was pushed back on Izard's head. It was one Austin had stuffed into the flour bag marked Izard. Next to him, Fergus was pulling a kerchief over his nose against the rising smoke. It had come from Kady's drawer.

We gave them everything they needed, and they're still acting like criminals! Austin thought.

"What you starin' at, boy?" Izard said. He jerked his shaggy head. "You ain't never seen a hat before?"

Yeah, Austin wanted to say. *I've seen a hat—that very one! Now give it back!*

"If I was you, I'd quit wishin' I had somethin' I ain't got and get on with puttin' out that fire," Izard said with an evil smile. He jerked his head again. "Did you get a good look at it? That there is a work of art."

"I'm surprised you knew how to spell it," Austin said coldly.

"We didn't," Fergus said. He held up a tattered piece of

paper. "Mr. Rhett done wrote it down for us."

"Shut up, Fergus," Izard snapped. "You heard what he said. We wasn't supposed to say nothin' if we was caught."

"Too late now," Austin said. "You're caught."

But Izard gave his colorless head one more snap and laughed. "No, we ain't. We're leavin' tomorrow with Mr. Rhett. You really think your highfalutin uncle is gonna come after us?"

"We got plenty more tricks like this if he does!" Fergus said.

Once more, Izard glared at him, but Austin knew he was right. Uncle Drayton had said it himself—he wouldn't strike back. If they didn't get the Wydells right now, they never would.

And no matter how much they had missed out on in their lives, they needed to pay for this.

"Good-bye, Yankee," Izard said from his stance atop the driver's seat. "Hey, too bad your face is healin' up so nice. You looked better when you was beat up. If we had time, I'd have Fergus here give you another go-round."

"Austin, where are you?" Kady shouted from afar. "We need help at the well!"

"Sounds like they're callin' you, Mr. A. T. Hutchinson," Izard sneered. "We'd best be gettin' out of your way."

He tugged on his hat and appeared to be ready to leave. Austin looked frantically around, but everyone was scattered, tending the fire. Uncle Drayton or Henry-James could stop them easily. He'd seen his uncle almost tumble Virgil Rhett himself from a wagon.

And then Austin remembered something. Without moving his mouth, he made a clicking sound with his tongue.

At once, the nervous horse lurched forward, yanking the

wagon behind him. Izard grabbed wildly at the air, but there was nothing there to catch him.

"Whoa!" Austin shouted.

The horse stopped, then in confusion backed up. Still flailing, Izard was hurled forward, and he toppled headlong out of the front of the wagon and onto the ground.

Fergus blinked down at him, mouth hanging open, ready for the next "huh." He was still staring at his brother when Uncle Drayton arrived.

I wanted a summer of picture-perfect moments, Austin thought several weeks later. *I've gotten only a few—but I'm not complaining, God.*

He rolled over from his spot on the grassy hill and surveyed the burn marks left by Izard and Fergus's handiwork. Wildflowers were already starting to grow back in. That was one.

He glanced up at the front porch and saw another one. His mother and Uncle Drayton were sitting there talking, the way they'd been doing a lot lately. Actually, Austin noticed that it was his mother who did most of the talking. Uncle Drayton sat looking studiously at his knees and nodding. Once Austin heard him say, "My heart is broken, Sally. I need your help."

With all these hearts broken, Austin thought, *I guess Jesus doesn't hand out too many picture-perfect moments, no matter how hard you wish.*

Austin sat up and squinted down the road. There was a carriage coming, kicking up dust on the road.

Who could that be? Austin asked himself. *I thought everybody hated us.*

The carriage stopped at the side of the house where the

steps were, and Henry-James hurried out to meet it. Austin took off down to the lake to find Charlotte.

"Mama has visitors?" she said when Austin told her. "Let's go spy."

By the time they crept back into the bushes below the side porch, Aunt Olivia was sitting there with a tea tray, entertaining two women. One had a little girl seated beside her, head down, swinging her legs.

Aunt Olivia was waving her jeweled, plump hands as she poured the tea and offered sandwiches and leaned, laughing, across the table.

"Thank you for saying that," Austin heard her say.

"It's true," said one lady. "Roger said Drayton was terribly brave to stand up to the men the way he did, and even though they are worlds apart in their beliefs, he thought it was only fitting that I should come call on you."

"That's Mr. Pryor's wife," Austin hissed.

"Well, I do thank you," Aunt Olivia said. For a second, Austin thought she was going to start sniveling. But she suddenly smiled generously and said, "Now then, tell me about that handsome son of yours, Miz Reed."

The other lady chuckled huskily. "All I can say is that Randall is quite taken with your daughter."

"My Kady?"

"No, Polly. Although he never says anything except 'Yes, Father' to his father, he confides in me. He said he thinks she's going to be quite a beauty when she comes into her own."

Charlotte stifled a snort. Austin made a mental note to tell Polly that later.

"Now, speaking of beautiful children," Aunt Olivia was saying to Susan Pryor, "where *did* you find this one?"

"Little Georgiana?" the woman said.

Austin and Charlotte stared at each other.

"Georgiana?" Charlotte whispered.

"Roger took her on with her brothers," Susan Pryor said, "only because they said there was no one in Greenville to look after her. But from the first day, I could see that she was nothing like those two scalawags. When Virgil Rhett sent them back—after the unfortunate incident here—I insisted she stay with me."

"You have her dressed beautifully," Aunt Olivia said, casting an admiring look at Georgiana's pink, lacy dress. "I would never have guessed she was a poor white."

"Now, it was the strangest thing. She just pulled this out of an old sack she had next to her bed. She must have brought it with her from Greenville."

Aunt Olivia leaned in for a closer look, and Charlotte tugged Austin's sleeve.

"That was one of my dresses!" she whispered in his ear. "I bet Mama doesn't even recognize it."

"Someone certainly had good taste," Aunt Olivia said. "I wish I could get my Charlotte to wear such things. I'm afraid she's a tomboy."

Charlotte rolled her eyes. "Come on," she whispered. "Let's go play."

But Austin couldn't quite go yet. He watched Georgiana, still swinging her legs and staring down at her lap. She didn't look like she was having a picture-perfect moment.

"Aunt Olivia?" he said, marching toward the porch.

Aunt Olivia fluttered her eyes toward the railing. "What is it, dear?"

"May Georgiana come and play with us?"

Georgiana shifted her huge hazel eyes toward him, and her face froze.

"We won't play rough or anything," Austin said quickly. "She won't even get dirty."

"See that she doesn't," Aunt Olivia said. "Run along, honey."

Georgiana looked as if she would rather walk off the side of Big Glassy Mountain than join them, but with a pleading look over her shoulder at Susan Pryor, she came to the front steps.

"Don't worry," Austin whispered to her. "We know you aren't like your brothers."

"We need another girl," Charlotte said. "There're way too many boys around here sometimes."

Georgiana blinked her big eyes at them and then looked down at the toes of her white patent leather shoes—with the bows on them.

"Can we go to our carriage first?" she said. "I have your rabbit in there."

Charlotte looked at her for only a minute before she put her arms around her neck. "No," she said. "You keep it."

It was a little bit sappy for Austin, but it might have been the most picture-perfect moment yet.

All right, Austin thought, *so maybe it's only the important ones that are perfect*. And having a whole afternoon with a new friend—now *that* was important.

✠ ❖ ✠

There's More Adventure in the CHRISTIAN HERITAGE SERIES!

The Salem Years, 1689–1691

The Rescue #1

Josiah and his older sister, Hope, used to fight a lot. But now, she's very sick. And neither the town doctor nor all the family's wishing can save her. Their only earthly chance is an old widow—a stranger to Salem Village—whose very presence could destroy the family's relationship with everyone else! Can she save Hope? And at what price?

The Stowaway #2

Josiah is going to town! Sent to Salem Town to be educated, Josiah Hutchinson's dream of someday becoming a sailor now seems within reach. But a tough orphan named Simon has other plans, and his evil schemes could get both Josiah and Hope in a heap of trouble. How will the kids prove their innocence? Whose story will the village believe?

The Guardian #3

Josiah has heard the wolves howling at night, and he's devised a way of dealing with them. But with the perfect night to execute the plan approaching, there's still one not-so-small problem—Cousin Rebecca, who follows Josiah around like his shadow . . . even into danger! How will Josiah protect her? What will happen to the wolves?

The Accused #4

Josiah Hutchinson is robbed by the cruel Putnam brothers! In a desperate attempt to retrieve his stolen property, he's accused of being the thief and unexpectedly finds himself on trial for crimes he didn't commit! Can Josiah find the courage to tell the truth? Will anyone believe him if he does? Will he be torn from his family and locked away in a dingy jail cell?

The Samaritan #5

Taking to heart a message he heard at church, Josiah attempts to help a starving old widow and her daughter. But while he's trying hard to forge new friendships, the feud with the Putnams is getting out of control. Will Josiah be clever enough to escape their wicked ways? Can God protect him when it seems hopeless?

The Secret #6

Hope's got a crush on someone—and Josiah knows who it is! Can he keep it a secret? After all, if Papa found out who she's been sneaking away to see, he'd be furious! And if the Putnams find out, who knows what will happen!

The Williamsburg Years, 1780–1781

The Rebel #1

The Hutchinson family history continues in the first book of the Williamsburg Years. Josiah's great-grandson, Thomas, doesn't think he'll ever like Williamsburg. Things get worse when the apothecary shop he works in is robbed! Thomas thinks he knows who did it, but before he can prove it, he's accused of the crime and taken to jail. How will he convince everyone he's innocent?

The Thief #2

Horses are being stolen in Williamsburg! And after Thomas sees a masked rider leading a horse, he believes it's Nicholas, the new doctor who has come to town. When Thomas's friend is seriously injured, Thomas knows the young doctor may be his friend's only chance. Can he trust Nicholas to take care of him?

The Burden #3

Thomas Hutchinson knows secrets, but he can't tell anyone! And he soon learns that "bearing one another's burdens," as he heard in church, is not always easy—especially when a crazed Walter Clark holds him at gunpoint for a secret he doesn't even know! Will Walter ever believe Thomas? How will he be freed of these secrets?

The Prisoner #4

War in Williamsburg is raging! But when Thomas's mentor, Nicholas, refuses to fight, he is carried off against his will by the Patriots. Witnessing this harsh treatment, Thomas feels confused and trapped. Whose side should he be on? Will he ever understand what it means to be free?

The Invasion #5

When word arrives that Benedict Arnold and his men are ransacking plantations nearby, Thomas, his family and friends return to their homestead to protect it. But British soldiers break in, taking food, horses and Caroline as hostage! Now what? Will Thomas be able to help straighten out this horrible situation?

The Battle #6

Though the war is all around him, Thomas is more frustrated by the *internal* fighting he feels. He's expected to take orders from a woman he doesn't like, he's forbidden to talk about his missing brother, Sam, and, to top it all off, he's not getting along with two of his closest friends. Will nothing turn out right?

The Charleston Years, 1860–1861

The Misfit #1

When the crusade to abolish slavery reaches full swing,

Austin Hutchinson (Thomas's great-grandson) is sent to live with relatives. But he's not sure he'll enjoy his stay because his cousins—Kady, Polly, and Charlotte—don't seem to like him. Even Henry-James, the slave boy, wants nothing to do with him. Will Austin ever find his place?

The Ally #2

When Austin discovers that Henry-James can't read, Austin resolves to teach him—even though it's illegal to educate slaves. But that only leads to trouble! Uncle Drayton is furious when he realizes Henry-James has secretly been given lessons and locks him in an old shack until he can be sold. Can Austin free Henry-James without getting them into more trouble? Will he able to forgive Uncle Drayton for being so harsh?

Available at a Christian bookstore near you

Here's a sneak peek at the next installment in
CHRISTIAN HERITAGE SERIES
THE CHARLESTON YEARS, Book #4
The Trap
Chapter One

"**M**assa Austin, what you doin'? Get your white self down from there 'fore all the blood rush to your head!"

Austin lifted his head of deer-colored hair from its up-side-down position in the oak tree and grinned down at his slave friend.

"I'm doing a scientific experiment, Henry-James," he said.

Thirteen-year-old Henry-James arched a dark eyebrow. "You tryin' to find out how long a boy can hang by his knees from a tree 'fore he faint dead away?"

Austin grinned again—and wondered how a smile looked upside down. "No," he said, pulling himself upright on the branch by his lanky arms. "I wanted to see how gravity looks backward. You know, if I dropped something, would it go up or down?"

From below him on the picnic cloth, three faces looked at him blankly. Bogie, Henry-James's blood-houndish mutt, shook his big, floppy-skinned head.

"What you talkin' 'bout, Massa Austin?" Henry-James said. "I don't know nothin' 'bout no gravity."

"What *is* gravity, Boston Austin?"

Austin dropped down beside 11-year-old Charlotte. She was cocking her head—with its hair the same color as his—and surveying him out of her quiet, golden-brown eyes, also the same color as his. In fact, almost everything about them was so much alike, they looked more like twins than cousins. The only difference was that Charlotte's hair cascaded over her shoulders, while Austin's was close-cropped around his ears and formed a wispy fringe across his forehead.

"I read a book about it," Austin said.

"Now tell me somethin', Massa Austin," Henry-James said. "Is there anything you *ain't* read a book about?"

Austin had to stop and think about that, which he did while pulling the last of the peppermint cakes out of the picnic basket. His little brother Jefferson's pudgy face pinched into a frown.

"Why do we gotta talk about gravididdy? We're supposed to be havin' a picnic."

"We're having it," Austin said, shoving most of the cake into his mouth.

Charlotte stretched out on the grass beside the cloth and tapped the toes of her high-topped, button-up shoes together. "This could be the last chance we have for a picnic," she said. "It's going to start getting cold soon."

"This been my *first* chance," Henry-James said.

"You've been working too hard," Austin said. "Doing all that harvesting and threshing, plus being Uncle Drayton's body slave."

"All that harvestin' and threshin' done now," Henry-James said. "And I thank the Lord for that."

Austin did, too. Ever since they had all come back from their summer in Flat Rock, North Carolina, he'd spent a lot of time watching Henry-James work. It was Henry-James's first year out in the fields, but he'd kept up with the best of them, standing shoulder high among the rice plants, harvesting the grain with a sickle-shaped rice hook, and putting it out to dry.

Austin, Charlotte, and Jefferson had perched in the trees for days, watching the slaves and the poor whites Uncle Drayton had hired to help tie the dried grain into sheaves and stack it on the flat boats to be taken to the threshing and pounding mill.

"Daddy 'Lias say *he* thank the Lord that Marse Drayton finally done got hisself a mill," Henry-James said now. "They used to like to kill theyselves doin' that all by the strength of they arms and the sweat of they brows."

For weeks they'd listened to the huge millstones rotate and the heavy pestles pound. Austin couldn't picture Henry-James and the others, men and women alike, doing all of that by hand, although Aunt Olivia had complained endlessly of a headache and said it was so much quieter the old way.

"But this brings in the money so much faster, my dear," Uncle Drayton had said to her with his usual charming smile. "You just think about that new French Victorian furniture that's on its way." His golden-brown eyes had twinkled. "That should cure your headache."

As far as Austin was concerned, Aunt Olivia *was* a headache.

"So what are we going to do now?" Jefferson said, peering into the empty picnic basket. "I'm bored."

"I could give you all a science lesson," Austin said. "Do

you know what the name of that tree is?"

"The one you was just danglin' from?" Henry-James said.

"That's a live oak, Boston," Charlotte said.

"Nope, it's a *Quercus virginiana.*"

Henry-James fingered the gap between his two front teeth. "I done lived at Canaan Grove all my life, Massa Austin, and I ain't never heard of no tree called no 'quirkus Virginia.' This here is South Carolina!"

"That's the Latin name," Austin said. "That butternut hickory over there? That's a *Carya cordipormis.*"

"Carry a what?" Jefferson said.

"Now let me ask you somethin', Massa Austin," Henry-James said. "What good them big fancy words gonna do you? I mean, besides makin' you sound smart, which we already knows you is anyway."

Austin shrugged happily. "I don't know. I just like knowing things. And you can never tell when a piece of information might come in handy. Like, I've been reading about inventions—you know, the cotton gin and the sewing machine and the steam engine. All of them came from knowing simple science."

"You sayin' by knowin' that there hickory tree be a carry-a-corpse, you could make you an invention, Massa Austin?"

"You talk about *me* being smart!" Austin said. "You almost got it, Henry-James! It's *Carya cordipormis—*"

"I don't care about that!" Jefferson said, flouncing himself around. "I want to do something *fun!*"

Since Jefferson's idea of fun was usually cornering a skunk or dumping a bucket of water over someone's head, Austin quickly scrambled for an idea. Before he got even a glimmer of one, Charlotte groaned, and Bogie lifted his big head and sniffed warily.

"What's wrong, Miz Lottie?" Henry-James asked.

Charlotte pointed across the lawn, where two figures were hurrying from the direction of the spring house toward the big plantation mansion. It was 17-year-old Kady, being held by the arm by her mother, Austin's Aunt Olivia, who as usual was wagging her elaborately piled head of dark hair while she scolded away. They could hear it even from there.

"Mr. Garrison McCloud is waiting in our parlor, and here you are dressed like a schoolmarm!"

"I *am* a schoolmarm, Mama!"

"You are nothing of the kind, and don't you dare tell Mr. McCloud that you are teaching our slaves to read! We are outsiders enough these days!"

Austin watched thoughtfully as they disappeared up the back steps and inside the Big House. "Who's Garrison McCloud?" he said.

"He's another beau Mama and Daddy lined up for Kady," Charlotte said. "She already met him at the Singletons' barbecue."

"Does she like him?" Austin asked.

"No, she says he's boring."

"I know about boring!" Jefferson said impatiently.

Charlotte's eyes began to sparkle. "But Polly likes him. That's all she talked about when we came home. 'Garrison smiled at me. . . . Garrison picked up my handkerchief.' "

Austin snorted. "Probably only because she threw it right on his toes!"

"Speakin' of the devil," Henry-James muttered.

Austin looked up and snorted again. Fourteen-year-old Polly was that very moment emerging from the back door, dressed in yellow with enough bows and lace and ribbons to clothe three girls. Her skirt swayed on its wide hoop so that only the dainty toes of her yellow shoes peeked out. Polly herself peeked out from under a wide-brimmed straw hat. Austin studied her carefully as she swept down the steps and paraded across the lawn.

"There's something different about her," he said.

"She ain't got Tot with her," Henry-James said.

That was true. It was odd to see Polly without her stump-shaped slave girl.

"That's because she wants to flirt with Kady's beau," Charlotte said, wrinkling her freckled nose. "Which I think is disgusting. But if she's going to do it, she can't have Tot around. She's likely to trip the boy!"

Austin shook his head. "But that isn't what's different about her. I think she looks . . . I don't know, *better*."

It was Charlotte's turn to snort. "She couldn't have looked worse!"

That was probably true, too. Poor Polly. Limp, brass-colored hair hung at her neck like wilted stems, refusing to go into curls no matter how many hours she made Tot work at it. Her eyes weren't quite brown and weren't quite green, so they blinked in the mire somewhere in between. Her too-skinny arms and legs always seemed to be flying out in four opposite directions. And worst of all, she had brown teeth. It was no wonder she didn't smile very much.

Austin's mother, Sally Hutchinson, said Polly was an almost-there version of her father, who was really quite handsome. "She'll grow into herself," Mother said whenever the topic came up. "Drayton was no beauty when he was that age, and neither was I. You just give her time."

"And prayer," Kady always added.

It wasn't surprising that Kady and Charlotte didn't give Polly much room. She'd always been her mother's pet, which meant she tattled on her sisters every chance she got. When Austin had first arrived last January, Polly had started in on him like he was a tiger's fresh meat—although he had to admit that he hadn't missed many chances to get back at her. But last summer, they'd called a truce, and she had started being nicer . . . at least as nice as Polly could be.

"That there must be Massa McCloud," Henry-James said.

They all looked toward the back door where Kady was stepping out, still in her gray-and-black striped dress with a net over her thick, dark hair. A young man barely an inch taller than she came out behind her. His hair was so blond that it was nearly blinding. He ran his hand carefully over it, perched his pearl-gray hat jauntily on it, and smoothed his waistcoat over his broad chest.

Bogie gave a low growl.

"You don't like that boy, Bogie?" Charlotte said, giggling.

"Ain't nobody good enough for Miz Kady, far as we sees it," Henry-James said. He breathed in until his nostrils flared. "If'n she don't like him, I hopes Marse Drayton don't make her marry him."

"*Make* her?" Austin said, twisting to look at Henry-James. "He wouldn't do that, would he?"

"He wouldn't have to force Polly," Charlotte said, pointing. "Look at that!"

Polly swirled around on the path toward the gardens and put her hand over her mouth. "Oh my, Kady!" she sang out. "I didn't see you there. Oh, and Mr. *McCloud!*"

" 'Mr. McCloud!' " Charlotte mocked her in a high-pitched voice. "Oh, please."

Garrison McCloud smiled an instant smile and held out his free arm to Polly. The three of them strolled off into the gardens and disappeared amid the crepe myrtles.

"At least he didn't chase Polly off like Kady's last beau did," Austin said.

"That was funny!" Charlotte said. "She didn't speak to Kady for days—which didn't bother Kady!"

"I'm still bored!" Jefferson said with a squall.

"You won't be bored tomorrow at the corn-husking party, Jefferson," Charlotte said. "Think about that."

"I don't even know what a corn-husking party is," Jefferson said. He folded his arms stubbornly across his chest.

"It's one of the best times of the whole year!" Charlotte said. "There's more food than you can even think about, and games and the husking, of course, which is fun."

"And don't be forgettin' 'bout the wrestlin'," Henry-James put in.

"Wrestling?" Austin said.

"There's a big wresting match to see who's the best on the plantation," Charlotte said. She grinned at Henry-James. "This is your first year!"

Henry-James nodded his woolly head and gave one of his rare smiles. "I been practicin' with Isaac and them."

"Isaac's the biggest slave at Canaan Grove!" Austin said. "Didn't he hurt you?"

"He just showin' me some tricks. We ain't gon' fight together. I be wrestlin' other boys same size as me."

"Like me," said a voice behind them.

They all turned to see a dark-haired boy leaning, cross-armed, against a palm tree several yards away. Austin had seen him before, working in Uncle Drayton's fields with his

father and brother. He'd thought then as he thought now:
*This boy has the tightest looking mouth I ever saw! It looks
like a line across his face.*

He also had a big head with one sliver of hair that
wouldn't join the rest of his combed-back thatch and fell
down over his high forehead. He stared at them now with
bright green eyes.

Henry-James stared back for a minute and then lowered
his gaze, the way he'd been taught to do around white
folks—except Charlotte, Kady, Jefferson, and Austin, who
considered him a friend. Charlotte, too, looked down at the
picnic cloth. She always did that around people she didn't
know . . . or didn't like.

That left Austin to do the talking. It was a job he didn't
mind much.

"I'm Austin Hutchinson," he said. "And you are—?"

The green eyes pointed like darts. "You ain't from
around here," the boy said.

Austin grinned. "Oh, you mean my accent. I'm from up
north. My mother and my brother and I are staying here for
a while because my father travels and my mother was too
sick to go with him."

"A Yankee," the boy said. His mouth tightened so hard
that Austin looked closely to see how he was going to talk
out of it. "I don't like Yankees," he muttered from the slit.

"Then I'm glad you're not going to wrestle *me*," Austin
said cheerfully. "Now Henry-James is a native South Caro-
linian, born right here in St. Paul's Parish—"

"I don't like darkies either."

"Then I don't like *you!*" Jefferson cried, getting up on
his knees and doubling his pudgy fists. His blue eyes were
blazing.

The boy ignored him and fixed his own green ones on Henry-James. "How 'bout you and me fight right now?" he said.

Charlotte looked up sharply, but Henry-James still stared at his knees.

Austin felt the first poking of irritation in his backbone. "It's all right, Henry-James," he said. "You can look at him. He's a worker, same as you."

"I ain't the same as him!" the boy shrieked. "I ain't one bit the same as him!"

And then he charged the picnic blanket and hurled himself onto Henry-James.

Charlotte cried out and scrambled up, dragging Jefferson with her. Austin crawled over to the struggling pair, shouting, "That isn't fair! You took him by surprise!"

His answer was an elbow in the face that knocked him backward and sent him rolling off the blanket.

"Stop!" Charlotte screamed. "Austin, make them stop!"

But Austin didn't even know where to start. With fists flying and legs wrapped around other legs, it was hard to tell where Henry-James left off and the white boy began.

Bogie seemed to know, though. With a juicy snarl, he hurled himself into the fray and chomped his teeth down on the boy's plaid shirt. Digging his front paws into the ground and poking his backside in the air, Bogie tugged, still growling. But the white boy didn't so much as slow down, even when his shirt ripped and Bogie tumbled backward.

"He's going to hurt Henry-James!" Charlotte cried. "He's going to kill him!"

But just then Henry-James emerged on top of the rolling pile of arms and legs and pinned the white boy flat on his back. He held his shoulders with both of his square hands and breathed down on him, nostrils flaring in and out like a blacksmith's bellows.

"Get him, Henry-James!" Jefferson shouted.

"Don't you do anything of the kind, boy!" a voice behind them trumpeted. "Or you will have me to reckon with!"